The Rancher's Baby

KATHY DOUGLASS

HARLEQUIN

**SPECIAL
EDITION**

Recycling programs for this product may not exist in your area.

ISBN-13: 978-1-335-72458-8

The Rancher's Baby

Copyright © 2023 by Kathleen Gregory

For questions and comments about the quality of this book, please contact us at CustomerService@Harlequin.com.

Harlequin Enterprises ULC
22 Adelaide St. West, 41st Floor
Toronto, Ontario M5H 4E3, Canada
www.Harlequin.com

Printed in U.S.A.

Kathy Douglass is a lawyer turned author of sweet small-town contemporary romances. She is married to her very own hero and mother to two sons who cheer her on as she tries to get her stubborn hero and heroine to realize they are meant to be together. She loves hearing from readers that something in her books made them laugh or cry. You can learn more about Kathy or contact her at kathydouglassbooks.com.

This book is dedicated with love
to my husband and sons. Thank you for
supporting me as I pursue my dreams.
I love you all more than words can ever express.

Prologue

Isaac Montgomery glanced at his watch and then rose from the sofa beside the window. Glancing quickly at the unobstructed view of the Chicago skyline, he returned to the reception desk. His flight from Denver to Chicago had been delayed by two hours and, as a result, he'd been an hour late for his meeting with Joel Wilson. He'd called the attorney when he'd realized he wouldn't be there at the appointed time and attempted to reschedule for a later date, but the lawyer—of Parker, Kendrick and Wilson—had insisted that the meeting was important and that he would squeeze Isaac in that afternoon.

Now, though, Isaac had been waiting close to forty-five minutes and was growing impatient.

Surely, they could reschedule this meeting until tomorrow and discuss this mysterious topic then.

"Excuse me, Jenna," he said to the receptionist who looked up at him. She was cute—and wore no rings on her fingers. If she wasn't busy tonight, maybe she'd be up for dinner and *whatever*. He would be in Chicago overnight and there was no reason to waste it by spending it alone. "Do you have any idea how much longer he will be?"

She smiled at him. "Let me check with Mr. Wilson's secretary."

He nodded and told himself to be patient while she spoke to someone on the phone. It wasn't as if he had plans for the evening. *Yet.*

"Mr. Wilson's secretary is on her way to get you now."

"Thank you."

A middle-aged woman in a blue dress and matching pumps, who introduced herself as Therese, greeted Isaac and then ushered him into a large office. The lawyer, a man of about forty, rose and circled an oak desk. He held out his hand for Isaac to shake. "Thank you for sticking around."

"I'm anxious to learn what this is all about. Your message was a little bit cryptic."

The man rubbed his chin ruefully. "Guilty as charged. But some things are better dealt with in person."

Isaac nodded in agreement. "Well, now that we're

face-to-face, I'm eager to hear what you have to say."

Mr. Wilson flashed a smile and then sobered. "Why don't you take a seat, Mr. Montgomery?" He gestured to a chair across from his desk, then returned to his own seat and rested his hands on a folder. "I don't know a way to tell you this other than straight-out. I'm sorry to inform you of the death your friend, Lisa Hooks."

The words pounded Isaac in the chest, stealing his breath. It was a moment before he could speak. "Lisa is dead? When? How?" *Why?*

"A week ago. She had cancer. An inoperable brain tumor. Unfortunately, her condition progressed faster than she and the doctors had anticipated."

The attorney paused, giving Isaac time to absorb the news. Isaac hated to think of Lisa dying alone, with only strangers to comfort her.

Lisa had been a private person, but she'd shared some details of her life with him years ago when she'd worked on his family's ranch, including the fact that she'd grown up in foster care. She'd had no family. His family had done all they could to make her feel welcome, including her in family meals and inviting her to spend holidays with them, as they did with all of their employees who didn't have relatives in the area. Despite their best efforts, Lisa had held them at a distance, only allowing them to get so close. Perhaps because she'd been in and out of other people's homes—and families—from birth, she wasn't willing to open her heart and allow herself to trust that they really considered her to be a part of their family.

For the most part, she'd kept her relationship with the Montgomery family strictly professional. Except with Isaac. She'd allowed him to get closer to her than his parents and brothers. Isaac and Lisa had spent hours together talking in the evenings after work. Lisa was beautiful and although she'd been five years older than him, he'd developed the biggest crush on her. When he'd been eighteen, he'd told her that he was going to marry her and give her the family she deserved. Lisa had laughed and told him to stick to girls his age. She'd liked the single life—and she noted that he did too.

He'd soon come to see that she was right. He wasn't the type to settle down. He always showed a woman a good time, but he'd been clear that a good time was all he was offering. He wasn't built for anything long-term. Luckily, despite his brief misstep, he and Lisa had been able to maintain their close friendship.

At least, he thought they had. Three years ago, she'd said it was time for her to move on. She'd promised to keep in touch with him, but after sending him a handful of cards at random times, always from different places, she'd seemed to drop off the face of the earth. He hadn't heard from her in nearly two years.

"I was Lisa's attorney," Mr. Wilson said, pulling Isaac back to the present. "When I learned of her death, I contacted you."

"I don't understand. Do they need someone to cover her final expenses?" Just saying the words broke his heart. Lisa would only be thirty now. That was too young to be dead. There was still so much life she needed to live. "I'll do that, of course."

"That's a generous offer. But she took care of that."

"Then I don't understand. I appreciate you giving me this news in person. But..." He shook his head, the thought vanishing before it was fully formed. "I'm sorry. I don't know what else to say."

"I understand. But I wanted to meet with you because of the baby."

Confusion swirled in. "What baby?"

"Lisa's. And yours."

"Mine? There has to be some mistake." His crush on Lisa hadn't been reciprocated. And then it had fizzled out. They'd never even kissed, much less slept together. There was absolutely no way that he could be the father of her child.

"Your name is on the birth certificate. Lisa gave me your information so that I could reach you. Which was good, because that keeps the baby from ending up in foster care."

He thought of Lisa and the little of her life that she'd shared with him. If she'd put his name on the birth certificate, she must have had a good reason. He knew that he was walking the thin line between the truth and a lie, but before he said anything, he needed to know more.

"I understand your surprise. She left a letter for you. Perhaps it will explain everything." Mr. Wilson rummaged through a file on his desk, pulled out a sealed envelope and handed it over. "I'll leave you alone to read."

Isaac nodded as he opened the envelope. Inside was a sheet of lined paper. He recognized Lisa's messy handwriting instantly—she'd always dashed off notes quickly, as if she didn't have time to waste, he'd once laughed to her. His vision blurred and he wiped his eyes on his sleeve.

Dear Isaac,

If you are reading this letter, that means you have just learned about Mia. I hope that you can forgive me for upending your life, but I have no choice. There is no one else.

You may be wondering about the biological father. Let's just say he would not be a good father to Mia. In fact, he doesn't even know she exists, and it is my wish that he never does. That's why I listed you as her father on her birth certificate. I know that was presumptuous on my part and I apologize. To be honest, I had expected to be around to care for her and you would never have to know what I did. Now, though, it should make things easier for the two of you to be together. If there was anyone I'd want to raise my daughter in my absence, it's you.

I remember the closeness of our friendship. Your desire to marry me. That wouldn't have worked for us, but I never forgot. Although you couldn't give me the family I never had, you can give that to my sweet little girl. And know that I'll forever be grateful.
Lisa

Isaac lowered the letter and closed his eyes. The love and concern that Lisa felt for her daughter was obvious in every word. He didn't quite understand what had made Lisa choose him, but she had. And he couldn't let her down.

"Did the letter clear up matters?" Mr. Wilson asked, stepping back into the room.

"Yes."

"Good." The attorney looked at him expectantly. "Do you have any questions?"

He swallowed his nerves and stood. "Just one. Where is my daughter?"

Chapter One

Isaac drove up to his parents' home, pulled into the driveway, and then cut the engine on his SUV. He leaned his head against the headrest and blew out a long breath. The past few days had been hectic, and he hadn't had a chance to process all that had happened. After the meeting with the lawyer, his head had been spinning. There hadn't been time to deal with his grief over Lisa's death or to absorb the fact that he was now the father of an eight-month-old girl.

Mr. Wilson, who'd insisted that Isaac call him Joel, had had Isaac complete a Voluntary Acknowledgment of Paternity Form, which Joel had later filed with the Department of Healthcare and Family Services. Isaac was now legally Mia's father. As far as he was concerned—with or without the government's agreement—he was her father in every way that mattered.

Joel had made a telephone call and then ushered Isaac out of his office to meet his daughter. Mia had been staying with Lisa's babysitter and her husband, who had two children of their own. The husband had given Isaac the third degree while the wife had held tightly to Mia as if willing to fight to keep her if Isaac didn't meet with her approval. At first, Isaac had been resentful of their attitude, but he soon began to appreciate their concern. Clearly, they cared for Mia and weren't willing to relinquish her to just anybody, even the person that Lisa claimed was Mia's father.

Isaac had spent thirty minutes telling Jeremy and Trisha about his life in Colorado. He'd shown them pictures of the ranch and his family. He wasn't sure what Lisa had told them about their supposed romance, or how it was that Mia had been conceived, so he hadn't mentioned that at all.

He must have said all of the right things because at the end of the conversation, Jeremy had shaken his hand and Trisha had settled Mia into his lap. Mia had taken one look at him and let out a large wail. Trisha had rushed back over, but Isaac had shaken his head, waving her away. If he was going to be a father, he needed to learn to comfort his child. Unfortunately, the only experience he had to go on was with his three-year-old nephew. Benji was a quiet child who loved being tossed into the air and wrestling in the grass. Isaac didn't think either would work with an eight-month-old girl.

He'd held the baby against his chest and began singing *You Are Not Alone*, the old Michael Jackson song and the first relaxing tune that came to mind. Rising, he'd begun to pace the room, jiggling her gently as he walked from window to door and back again. Eventually, she'd quieted and he counted that as a victory.

Trish watched quietly before sharing information about Mia's schedule as well as her likes and dislikes. She packed all of the baby's belongings and set them beside the front door.

"I'm going to miss this little sweetheart," Trish said, wiping a tear from her cheek. Her husband wrapped his arm around her, gave her shoulder a gentle squeeze and brushed a kiss against her temple.

"I would like for your family to remain a part of Mia's life," Isaac said, surprising himself. "I can't promise to get back to Chicago often, but you're welcome to come to Aspen Creek and visit her. We have plenty of room on the ranch, so you don't need to worry about a place to stay."

"Thank you," Trish said. "We'd like that very much."

They exchanged numbers and then Jeremy helped Isaac load Mia's belongings into the car. Fortunately, Mia had grown comfortable with him and she hadn't made a fuss when they'd left. The flight home had been smooth and uneventful, a welcome change after the whirlwind that had blown through his life.

"We're home," Isaac said as he opened the rear passenger door. Mia looked at him while she chewed happily on her pacifier. Before leaving Chicago, he'd stopped by Lisa's apartment and gathered Mia's clothes and toys. He'd arranged for Lisa's belonging to be packed and shipped to the ranch. He'd deal with them later.

Looking at his parents' house, he realized just how much he needed his family and what Lisa had been deprived of in her lifetime. That feeling only solidified his determination to give Mia the family she needed. The family that Lisa had so wanted her to have. The very reason Lisa had chosen *him*.

He noted with satisfaction that his brothers' cars were already parked in the circular driveway. Miles, his older brother, lived with his son in a house on the east side of the ranch. He was engaged to marry the love of his life, and Jillian and her daughter, Lilliana, would be moving in with Miles and Benji after the wedding. Since Jillian was practically family, Isaac had requested that she attend this family meeting too. Isaac's oldest brother, Nathan, had a home on the ranch, although he spent so much time on the road the house sat deserted most of the time.

Isaac removed Mia from her car seat, slung the diaper bag over his shoulder and nudged the car door closed. Mia grinned at him, showing off four tiny teeth. Dimples flashed in her cheeks that were reminiscent of Lisa's, and pain stole his breath. Why hadn't Lisa told him she was sick? He would have brought her home where she would have been loved and cared for.

"Oh, oh, oh," Mia chanted, shaking him out of his reverie.

"Right," Isaac replied as he climbed the stairs. Although he had been devastated to find out about Lisa's death, in the end, Joel had been right to summon him to Chicago to tell him in person. Telling him over the phone would have been insensitive—and he couldn't even imagine how he'd have reacted to learning about Mia that way. He knew he had to be as courteous to his family, who'd loved Lisa and would be hurt to learn of her sudden death.

He stepped inside the house. Laughter and conversation floated on the air from the kitchen, mingling with the delicious aromas of his mother's cooking. He followed the sound and the scents to the back of the house. His family was congregating in the kitchen and the adjoining family room. His mother looked up from her place at the granite center island and paused. Her eyes went from his face to Mia and her welcoming smile turned to a confused one. Conversation faded away until there was complete silence, and everyone stared at him.

"Who do we have here?" his mother asked as she circled the large island and approached him.

"This is Mia." Isaac had rehearsed an entire speech, designed to carefully explain the situation, but it deserted him now. So he cut to the chase. "My daughter."

"Your what?"

There was a burst of conversation as everyone talked at once. The sudden noise frightened Mia, who whimpered and clung to his shirt.

Michelle held up a hand, silencing everyone. "Let Isaac talk."

"Thanks, Mom." He removed Mia's jacket and then took a seat at the kitchen table, holding her on his lap. She instantly reached for the crystal fruit bowl in the middle of the table, and he quickly pushed the bowl out of her grasp. He was still learning just how fast she could move.

"You're welcome. Now, do you want to explain what you meant by *your daughter*?"

He nodded. "Do you remember Lisa Hooks? She worked as a ranch hand?"

"Of course," his mother said. "She was such a nice young lady. I hated to see her go."

"Mia is her daughter. Sadly, Lisa died recently and, according to her attorney, she wanted me to raise Mia."

"Lisa *died*?" Miles said, shock creeping into his tone.

"Oh no," Michelle said, her hand pressed against her mouth.

"That's terrible," Isaac's father said. Edward pulled Michelle into an embrace and rubbed her back.

There was silence as everyone absorbed the news. After a while, conversation resumed.

"She named you as Mia's guardian?" Nathan's voice was filled with shock and disbelief. For some unknown reason, that annoyed Isaac.

"Why wouldn't she? We were very close."

"Were you sleeping with her?"

"No," Isaac said. "Not that that is any of your business."

"Have you been in touch with her?" Edward asked, diffusing the situation between Isaac and Nathan before it got out of control.

"No," Isaac replied. "I haven't spoken to her in years."

"You're single," Nathan pointed out as if Isaac was unaware of that fact.

"Miles has been a single father for years and nobody questions his ability to raise Benji on his own."

"Miles is Benji's biological father," Nathan said.

"And that makes it different how?" Isaac said. "Biology doesn't automatically give him special skills."

"We're getting off track here, so let's stick to the topic," his mother said. Michelle looked around the room, a stern expression on her face. She might only be a shade over five feet, but nobody dared challenge her when she made a serious declaration. "Continue your story."

"There's not much more to say," Isaac said and then hesitated. "That's not entirely true. She left me a letter where she explained that she listed me as Mia's father on the birth certificate. I have it with me if anyone wants to read it. I filed a Voluntary Acknowledgment of Paternity form, making me her legal father."

There was silence for a moment while his family digested his words. Then there was a second round of chaos that he ignored. Finally, his father got everyone quieted down and Isaac continued. "I didn't expect it, but I know Lisa had her reasons. And I'm fine with it. I told you about Mia's paternity because you're my family and deserve to know the truth. But as far as the rest of the world knows, Mia is my child."

"So you intend to raise her?" Nathan asked. Once more his voice was filled with disbelief.

Isaac frowned, tamping down his annoyance. "Yes. I thought I had been clear on that."

"I know that's what you said. But you're not like Miles. No offense," Nathan said, being offensive. "You're not the family type. You're with a different woman every night. And now you want us to believe that all of a sudden you're going to settle down in order to become a father? To someone else's child?"

Although no one seconded Nathan's comment,

Isaac noted that none of his family jumped to his defense either. He had spent his free nights partying in the past. He was twenty-five and single after all. But that was before he had a child. But he didn't bother pointing that out. Nothing he said would convince them that he could be a good father. Only actions would do that.

"I don't care what you believe. I know there are things in my life that need to change. And I'm willing to make those changes to be the type of father that Mia deserves. The type of father we had. You're going to be part of her family too. It's my hope that you'll love her as much as you love Benji and Lilliana."

"One thing has nothing to do with the other."

In other words, he still thought Isaac was going to be a lousy father.

"Being a parent is hard work," Michelle said. "Especially when you're jumping in without warning or experience."

"I know. That's one of the reasons I asked all of you to come here today. I know I'm going to need my family's support. But regardless of the naysayer—" he looked at Nathan who stared back at him "—I am going to do this."

"We'll help in any way that we can," Edward said. "Now that that's settled, I want to hold my new grandbaby," Michelle said.

Isaac handed over Mia and then watched as his

mother cuddled and kissed her. Isaac felt a hand on his shoulder and looked into Miles's face. His brother was smiling.

"Congratulations. If you need any tips, just ask."

"Thanks." Isaac had overcome the first hurdle in getting Mia home to Colorado and introduced to his family, but he knew there would be many more in the future. It was comforting to know that his family—with the exception of Nathan—would be on his side. He didn't delude himself. He knew they probably had doubts too. But he was grateful that they were willing to let him prove himself rather than judging him as incapable of changing his ways and being a good father.

Savannah Rogers walked down the empty streets of Aspen Creek, Colorado, oblivious to the gorgeous surroundings. It was early spring, and although it had been in the midfifties earlier, the temperature had dipped a bit once the sun set, so she wound the scarf around her neck, letting the ends trail over the front of her coat. The moon was bright in the night sky, providing enough illumination for her to make out the line of the Rockies in the distance. Aspen Creek was a popular resort town and people came from far and wide to ski and enjoy outdoor sports and activities. During the day, it bustled with locals and tourists. The last thing Savannah wanted was to interact with people, which was why she avoided coming to town in the daytime hours.

But at night, it was quiet. Peaceful. Deserted. Just what she was looking for. All she wanted in life was to be left alone. No, that wasn't true. What she really wanted was the same thing she'd wanted for the past four hundred and thirty-seven days.

She wanted her husband and three-year-old son back.

But since that was impossible, she went with the next best thing. Solitude.

That was why she'd left her home in Madison, Wisconsin, and moved to Colorado. Moving hadn't been something she'd put a lot of thought into. She'd just known that she couldn't stay in the house one more day without Darren and their sweet son, Tony. So, six weeks and three days after their funeral, she'd taken leave from her job as an English Literature professor at UW Madison, put her house up for sale, gotten into her car and driven away. She hadn't had a destination in mind. She'd simply driven until she'd gotten tired of being behind the wheel of the car and then found a hotel to stay in overnight. The next morning, she'd started the process again.

When she'd reached Aspen Creek, she'd stumbled upon a cabin for rent. It was out of the way and far enough from town that she wasn't at risk of running into people too often. There was a cattle ranch nearby, but she had yet to encounter any of the ranchers. All in all, she was able to live quietly on her own. Maybe some wouldn't understand it—most people did tend to seek company, she knew that well.

But she didn't want any. She was, if not content, at least in a rhythm that worked—for her, anyway.

After walking through the empty town, she returned to her car and drove to the big-box store near the highway. At this time of night, there would be very few people there and they wouldn't be any more interested in making small talk than she was. Anyone who was there now wanted to get in, grab what they needed, and get out as quickly as possible.

Savannah had a system and generally was able to get through her entire shopping list in thirty-seven minutes. She bought the same items each time, and knew which aisles to walk down to grab what she wanted. She'd been shopping for eighteen minutes when she turned into the laundry detergent aisle. A muscular man with shoulder-length black locks with blond tips was standing in the middle of the aisle, holding two bottles of detergent in his hands as if debating which one to buy.

Savannah was standing in front of the fabric softener, so she could have picked up the bottle she needed, turned her cart around and left. Instead, she watched as the man set one bottle on the shelf and then read the back of the other one. When he was finished, he exchanged bottles and repeated the process. Then he grabbed his phone and, for a second, she wondered if he was going to call someone for advice. As it was already past midnight, she certainly hoped not. Then she watched as he stared at the screen. It dawned on her then that he was googling information. She didn't know why that made her smile when nothing else in the world could, but it did.

At that moment, he glanced in her direction. In profile, he was attractive. Straight-on, he was positively gorgeous. When he saw her smile, he returned it with one of his own, then seemed to hesitate as if remembering something. He turned and grabbed the shopping cart that he had been blocking. He spun it around and her eyes immediately went to the baby sitting there. The girl looked to be about nine or ten months old. She was looking around the store with alert eyes as she gnawed on a teething ring. Just the sight of the child made Savannah's heart ache.

She needed to get away from the father and daughter duo. Before she could make her escape, the baby let out a loud cry and tossed her teething ring on the floor. The man instantly reached for the baby, who began to cry in earnest. The man picked up the child and began singing an R & B ballad. He had a nice baritone voice, but the baby wasn't soothed. Everything in Savannah urged her to flee, but her feet resisted. When they finally did move, they went toward the man and baby instead of away.

"It looks like you need help," she heard herself say. She picked up the teething ring and handed it to the man.

"That's the understatement of the night. I'm trying to figure out the right laundry detergent to use. The ratings on the mom blogs I've been following are all over the place and there is no general consensus."

Savannah glanced at the shelf and instinctively picked up a bottle of the brand she'd used when Tony was a baby. "Either would be good, but I would go with this one."

He took the bottle from her and set it into his cart. "Thanks. I guess I was taking too long and Mia got a bit impatient."

His words brought back painful memories of Tony. She remembered how easily he could flip between contentedly entertaining himself and becoming upset and demanding her immediate attention at that age. She would give anything to go back in time and be able to hug her precious son once more, no matter how fussy he was. Because of one drunk driver, she would never hold her sweet little boy in her arms again.

The baby girl glanced at her as if trying to decide if she liked her. Then she sniffed and gave a dimpled smile. She was adorable. And so huggable. Savannah needed to get away from her. From both of them.

Savannah chose to do her shopping in the middle of the night specifically to avoid people. Especially babies. Yet she'd come face-to-face with one.

"I've seen you around," the man was saying. "You're living in the cabin on the Duncan ranch. It's nice to finally meet you. I'm Isaac."

The baby blew out spit bubbles and then laughed. Isaac smiled and reached out to wipe her chin.

Savannah froze. *I can't do this.*

She knew she should introduce herself, but suddenly she couldn't breathe much less talk. She forced herself to inhale and aimed a finger over her shoulder. "I need to go."

Before he could reply, she turned and raced from the aisle, leaving her cart behind. She didn't slow down until she was sitting in her car. Then she lowered her head onto the steering wheel and cried.

Isaac watched as the woman darted from the aisle. He took a couple of steps in her direction and then stopped. What was he doing? The woman had run away from him, so the last thing he should do was chase her. Clearly, she was distressed about something. Had he done something to upset her so badly she'd run off without her groceries?

He replayed the interaction, starting from the instant she'd stepped into the aisle. Although he'd been comparing ingredients on infant laundry detergent, he'd caught a glimpse of her from the corner of his eye. She had curly shoulder-length black hair that she'd held back with a headband, clear brown skin, bright brown eyes and full, kissable lips. Even without a speck of makeup, she was absolutely stunning.

Past Isaac would have approached her immediately and done his best to charm his way into her life. But present Isaac was a single father who couldn't bring home every sexy woman who caught his eye. Those days were over and wouldn't be coming back anytime soon.

But when the woman had come over to him, Isaac had seen no reason to be rude. Hopefully, he hadn't come across as either too standoffish or too forward. After he reviewed every word they'd said to each other, he was just as confused as before. He had no clue what had gone wrong.

Though this was the first time Isaac had interacted with her, he'd seen her several weeks ago when he'd been leaving a club. She'd been at a distance, but he'd recognized her solitary figure. Even then, something about the woman had called to him.

A couple of days ago, he'd spotted her again, this time near the property line the Montgomery and Duncan ranches shared. He'd known someone had been renting the Duncan cabin for months, but when he'd finally caught a glimpse of her, she'd seemed so mysterious that his interest had been piqued and he'd wanted to get to know her. Learn more about her—who she was. Where she'd come from. Why she was staying in town...

Well, he'd certainly blown that. Too bad he didn't know how.

Mia's bad mood had passed, so he settled her into the cart.

He'd managed on his own for the past two weeks. Barely. He'd brought the same brand of baby food that Lisa had in her pantry and Mia had eaten it without complaint. He hadn't seen laundry detergent in Lisa's laundry room, so he'd been on his own there. And Mia was running out of clean clothes. Thankfully his neighbor had come along. Crisis averted.

Finished with his list for now, he started down the aisle when he passed the abandoned shopping cart. He couldn't just leave it there. Sighing, he grabbed the cart with his left hand and his cart with his right. Thankfully, there was no one in the checkout line and he was able to unload both carts right away. Mia looked on with interest as he worked. She kicked her legs occasionally, but for the most part, she was content to suck her thumb and observe the world around her.

Isaac checked his watch. Ten to one. In the beginning, Mia had slept through the night. Lately she had begun staying up later. He hadn't expected her to turn into a night owl. Had she learned that from him? She wasn't old enough to go to school, so did it really matter if she preferred the moonlight and stars to the sun? If the past couple of nights were any indicator, she'd conk out in about thirty minutes. That gave him plenty of time to stop by his new neighbor's cabin and deliver her groceries. Nothing in her cart would spoil if it sat outside overnight.

"We're going to make a little detour," he said to Mia. He'd read that talking to babies encouraged them to speak so he'd begun talking to her about everything.

"Ba to ma," Mia replied and then laughed.

Isaac didn't know what was funny, but he laughed too.

Once he had Mia secured in the SUV and the groceries stowed in the back, he headed for the highway that led to ranch country.

"The lady we just met lives on the ranch next to ours. I know she's been living there for a while because I saw smoke from the cabin's chimney over the winter. I wonder why I haven't seen her around more."

Mia babbled a response. Clearly, she'd been wondering the same thing too.

When he reached the Duncan ranch, he turned onto the long driveway. He passed the main house and continued on until he reached the isolated cabin where the mystery woman was staying. There was a car parked beside the stairs, so he knew someone was home. He grabbed the bags holding the items she'd selected, as well as the chocolate bars he'd grabbed at the last minute, and set everything near the door.

He walked quietly back down the stairs, thinking about her. Although this hadn't been the way he'd planned to meet his intriguing neighbor, it was better than nothing. After the way she'd lit out of the store, he wondered if she would be interested in being friends. He hoped so, but he knew the next move would have to be hers.

He just hoped it wasn't long before she made it.

Chapter Two

Savannah awoke the next morning and closed her eyes against the sunlight. She wasn't ready to face another day without her family, but sadly she had no choice in the matter. Forcing herself to get up, she immediately made her bed and then took a long hot shower before pulling on jeans and a long-sleeved shirt. The clothes fit loosely on her, but that was what happened when you lost your appetite.

That thought reminded her that she hadn't gotten her shopping done last night. She cringed as she recalled how she'd left the cart and run from the store without her groceries. Unbidden, she thought of Isaac and his little girl. Her dimpled smile reminded Savannah of her sweet Tony, and had managed to wring out tears that Savannah had been holding back.

Savannah loved the smell of the morning air, so she stepped onto the porch. And gasped. Several bags were sitting beside her front door.

"What in the world?" She opened a bag and peered inside. It took a moment for her to realize that these were the items she'd left behind at the store last night. That realization had her sinking to the porch chair, the bag of groceries at her feet.

There was only one explanation. Isaac had bought her groceries and then left them for her. Why would a virtual stranger—one with a fussy baby at that—go out of his way for her? His kindness was nearly her undoing. She had forgotten that generous people still existed. She wasn't willing to allow him into her world—she still needed her solitude—but her heart was warmed by his kindness.

She brought the bags inside and began to unload them. Her grief had sent her on the run in the midst of shopping, so she knew there were still items she needed to buy. But thanks to Isaac, she had some of her necessities.

She reached inside the last bag and pulled out a chocolate bar. That hadn't been in her cart. Smiling, she looked inside and saw four more. Why had Isaac thought to include them? Once more, she was filled with an unfamiliar sense of if not joy, then well-being.

She ripped open the wrapper on the one in her hand and took a big bite. Sweet and delicious. She closed her eyes and savored the taste. Just what the doctor ordered. Though her problems wouldn't vanish, the candy provided some comfort. It had been so long since she'd treated herself to anything, the candy felt like a gift.

Savannah set the teapot on the stove and then quickly put away her groceries. She made a cup of chamomile tea, grabbed the remains of the chocolate bar and went back into the living room. The cabin wasn't at all what she'd expected when she'd rented it sight unseen. She'd pictured a rustic one-room log cabin with a massive stone fireplace, scarred furniture and a utilitarian bathroom. The exterior of the place was indeed made of logs and there was a slate fireplace in the living room, as well as in each of the bedrooms, but that was where the similarity to her vision ended.

This fully furnished cabin was actually a modern three-bedroom that the owners used as a guesthouse. The enormous living room opened to an airy dining room. The gourmet kitchen came complete with granite countertops and backsplash and a huge center island. The bedrooms resembled rooms in a boutique hotel. The main bedroom had a spalike bathroom and had direct access to the deck with its hot tub, in-ground pool and sensational view of the Rockies. Someone else might have been impressed, but Savannah couldn't care less about the amenities. To her, its biggest selling feature was its lack of memories.

Leaning back in the rocking chair beside the window, Savannah savored the chocolate one square at a time, allowing her mind to wander. Doing so was a risky proposition because inevitably it returned to Darren and Tony. She missed them so much and mourned the happy life they'd shared that had been cut short. Her grief was a living, breathing being, walking beside her as she stumbled through her waking hours and whispering in her ear while she tossed and turned in her bed.

Surprisingly, now it wasn't images of her husband and son that she saw when she closed her eyes. Instead, it was Isaac. She pictured his handsome face and his friendly smile. The way his muscular body filled out his T-shirt. She wasn't sure whether to be relieved or disturbed by that development.

Clearly, she had too much time on her hands.

When only the dregs of her tea remained and the chocolate bar was a sweet memory, she rose and went to the kitchen to prepare her small breakfast of two slices of bacon and a piece of toast and sat on the back deck to eat.

When she was done, the rest of the day stretched interminably before her. She considered going back to the store and buying the rest of the items she needed, but quickly quashed that idea. Thanks to her sugar rush, she might be feeling more chipper than normal, but that feeling only got her so far. She didn't have it in her to interact with anyone today. She just needed to find something to fill her time.

Savannah smiled ruefully. She lived in one of the most beautiful places in the state if not the country. There were acres and acres of land where she could walk without running into another soul. All without leaving the property.

Savannah wasn't looking for a home. She was simply looking for a place to lay her head until... Well, she wasn't sure until what. Until she was ready to move on? Until the crippling pain went away? Until she was ready to move back to Madison and pick up the broken threads of her life? She shuddered at the thought. The idea of returning to the place she'd lived with Darren and Tony stole the breath from her lungs. She couldn't imagine traveling the streets of town where they'd walked side by side or going to college football games and cheering for the Badgers until she was hoarse. She didn't know where she would go next, but she knew she could never return to a place that was filled with reminders of what had been taken from her.

She cleared her mind, grabbed a jacket and stepped outside. She walked across the paved patio and, after a moment, headed east. The weather was pleasant, and the sun warmed her skin. She lifted her head and watched as birds soared across the cloudless sky until they were out of sight. Rabbits raced across the grass, oblivious to her presence. In the distance, deer frolicked, running in and out of the bushes.

She'd lived in a college town all of her life, so all of this nature was foreign to her. It was as if she'd wandered onto a nature reserve. There was something magical about this place that gave her a sliver of peace that had eluded her everywhere else. When she was outside, she was in her own little world where her painful reality couldn't intrude.

After fifteen or so minutes, she realized that wasn't the case today. Thoughts of Isaac and Mia played at the edges of her mind, disturbing her peace. No matter how hard she tried to banish them, they returned. She'd managed to keep her emotions under lock and key from the moment she'd lost Darren and Tony. She hadn't felt anything in four hundred and thirty-eight days. Now, despite her best efforts to contain her feelings, she felt a hint of unwanted attraction toward Isaac. She didn't know how she would manage it, but she was determined to squash all thoughts and feelings for him before they got out of hand.

Isaac stepped into his parents' house and went directly to the kitchen. Miles and Benji were there and the four of them were eating breakfast.

"Hi, Uncle Isaac," Benji said. He smiled brightly

before shoveling scrambled eggs into his mouth, ignoring those that spilled onto his shirt.

"Hi."

"I was hoping you'd stop by for breakfast," Michelle said, coming to her feet. "How do you want your eggs?"

"You don't have to cook anything special for me," Isaac said. "I can eat the scrambled eggs that you already cooked."

"They're cold."

"So I'll pop them into the microwave."

"In that case, let me hold my grandbaby."

"Don't you want to finish eating?"

"I can eat with one hand. Now, give me the baby."

"Yes, ma'am."

Isaac handed over his daughter, grabbed a plate and then filled it with bacon, scrambled eggs, grits and biscuits. Isaac hadn't been much of a breakfast eater in the past, but ever since Mia had come into his life, he'd begun joining his parents a few times a week. He wanted her to be comfortable with her family.

Although he had wanted to do it all on his own, he'd soon seen the error of that kind of thinking. Taking care of a child was hard. Doing it alone, even more so. He and Mia definitely needed a village. Fortunately, his family had opened their hearts and arms. Especially his mother, who was thrilled to have a little girl to spoil. She'd gone on a major shopping spree, buying countless little dresses and frilly outfits. He had to admit that Mia looked as cute as could be when his mother styled her hair with bows and barrettes.

Now he watched as his mother set Mia into a high chair and set a plastic plate of scrambled eggs in front of her. Isaac smiled. Michelle really was in her element. Mia immediately grabbed the spoon and aimed for her mouth. A few eggs made it inside, but most were smeared onto her face. In between smearing and chewing, she pounded on the high chair and scooted around in her seat. Clearly, she was enjoying her eggs more than she'd liked the oatmeal he'd tried unsuccessfully to get her to eat.

"Are you coming to playgroup?" Miles asked.

"I don't know. Don't you think Mia is a little young for that?"

Miles had told Isaac about the playgroup a few days ago. Preschoolers and toddlers, accompanied by their parents, met at the library to play and then listen to a story. Miles brought Benji every week and Jillian brought Lilliana. In fact, that was how Miles and Jillian, former high school sweethearts, had reconnected and rekindled their love.

"No. It's for little kids. It takes place in a large room and there's a separate area for kids Mia's age. Besides, you'll be there by her side. And it's a good opportunity for her to meet other kids and play.

Not that she is in need of toys," Miles said with a smart-ass grin.

Isaac laughed. Michelle had bought several toys for Benji to play with, but she'd gone overboard with Mia. The large family room resembled a toy store. There were dolls, big and small stuffed animals, and all kinds of musical toys. There was even a dollhouse that was taller than Mia. She wouldn't be able to play with it for a while, but that hadn't stopped his mother from purchasing it.

"Go ahead and take her," Michelle encouraged Isaac. "If she doesn't like it, then you can leave."

That was true. He had given Mia a family, and as great as that was, he knew that having friends could only enrich her life. Not that he expected her to find a best pal at her age. "All right. I guess we'll give it a try."

"Nice. It'll be good to have another man there."

Isaac laughed. "Being outnumbered by women is never a bad thing. Besides, isn't Jillian there? I imagine that you spend a lot of time with her."

"I do. And don't think about horning in on our time together."

"The thought never crossed my mind."

"Good."

"Until now."

Miles frowned. "There are a few single mothers there. Heck, Veronica is single. Maybe set your sights on her."

"Who's Veronica?"

"The children's librarian."

Isaac shrugged. "That means nothing to me."

"She was in Nathan's grade in school."

"Still nothing." Not that it mattered. He wasn't interested in a woman. No, that wasn't true. He couldn't stop thinking about the woman he'd met in the grocery store last week. Although their brief conversation had ended abruptly, she'd made a big impression on him. He just wished he knew what had sent her running away.

After breakfast, Isaac and Miles got into their respective SUVs and drove to the Aspen Creek library. Miles introduced Isaac to Veronica, who gave him a form to complete. When he was done, he and Mia joined the playgroup and Isaac looked for age-appropriate toys for her to play with.

Isaac sat her on a mat with a few large plastic toys and squatted beside her. She gave him a quizzical look and then grabbed a yellow tractor. He'd learned that she enjoyed musical toys and he'd bought quite a few of them. Sometimes he had more than one going at a time, which seemed to delight her as much as the cacophony got on his nerves. But she was his little girl, and her happiness was more important than his.

When she tired of the tractor, she scrambled across the mat to a brightly colored toy. He resisted the urge to help her and was rewarded by her proud smile when she reached her goal. Sitting up, she banged on the purple square painted with a cow. In an instant, the sound of mooing filled the air. She giggled and then pushed down the green pig, who oinked. Apparently, that was the funniest thing she'd ever heard because she laughed and hit the pig again. And again.

"I think we have a winner," Jillian said, sitting beside him.

Isaac grimaced. "I hope this doesn't mean we're going to have to become pig farmers."

"I don't think it's that serious."

"Where's Lilliana?"

"Have you forgotten how independent my child is? When we stepped inside, she grabbed Benji's hand and waved 'bye. When I stood there, she pointed at the door."

Lilliana might only be two, but she knew her own mind. Once, Isaac would have laughed at the idea of Jillian being banished by her daughter, but now that he had a little one of his own who'd stolen his heart, it wasn't quite as amusing. He couldn't imagine how badly it would hurt if Mia didn't want him around. "Wow. I'm sorry."

Jillian laughed. "Why? Because she wants to play with her friend? I'm glad she's as confident as she is. Besides, it's not as if she can drive home without me."

"I know," Isaac said and shook his head. What

was wrong with him? First, he couldn't stop thinking about the mysterious woman even though they'd only met once. Now, he was worried that Mia wouldn't need him. That was some first-class foolishness considering she wasn't even potty-trained. Becoming a father was changing him in ways he hadn't expected.

"Dadadada," Mia said, crawling over to sit on his lap.

He grinned and kissed her cheek.

Miles came over and joined them. "I told you not to monopolize my woman."

"She sought me out," Isaac said with a laugh.

"I can't imagine why."

"My innate charm? My good looks? Take your pick."

Miles snorted. Isaac smothered a yawn.

"Sleepy?" Jillian asked.

Isaac nodded. "Mia wakes up at least once a night crying. I change her diaper, but she won't go back to sleep unless I hold her on my lap in the rocking chair and sing to her. Then it's usually another hour or so before I can fall back to sleep."

He wouldn't mention that if she didn't wake up, he got up just to be sure that she was okay. Either way, he wasn't getting a full night's rest.

"She'll grow out of this phase," Jillian assured him.

"When?" Isaac asked and then yawned again. "The endless sleepless nights are catching up with me."

"I can't believe you're the same man who partied all night with the ladies and worked the next day." Miles said.

"It was only on the weekends. And it seems like a lifetime ago," Isaac admitted. "I can't imagine hanging out all night now."

"Parenthood will change you," Miles said.

Isaac nodded. He used to have to drag Miles out of the house for a little bit of guy time. Now he was the one spending every waking minute with Mia or worrying about her. Of course, his new neighbor had been occupying his thoughts lately. He'd gladly give up sleep to be with her.

"Story time," Veronica announced.

Miles and Jillian excused themselves to help their kids put away their toys so they could hear the story.

Isaac wasn't sure what to do, but he noticed two other mothers with infants joined the circle, holding their children on their laps, so he did the same.

Veronica read a story about a frog and his friend. Mia didn't appear to be interested, but the other kids, who'd been making a good deal of noise earlier, were quiet, listening in rapt attention. When Veronica reached the last page, the kids applauded. Mia joined in, clapping her little hands as she grinned up at him.

When the playgroup ended, he walked beside Isaac, Jillian and their kids to the parking lot.

"What did you think?" Jillian asked.

Isaac shrugged. "It was okay, I guess. But Mia might be a little bit young for this group. She didn't play with anyone and we have toys at home."

"I know. But it was good for her to be around other kids. It will help her to become more social."

"She has Benji and Lilliana."

"Yes, she does. But she's going to need more than them. She's going to need friends. I'm not saying you need to come every week. Just know that there will be friends here for her when you feel like she's ready. And if playgroup isn't for you, there are plenty of other activities to consider."

Isaac nodded. Aspen Creek might be a resort town, but there were plenty of activities for the locals, especially the children. There were regular festivals, street fairs and carnivals that he'd previously ignored. Now he'd need to start paying attention to the fliers around town.

"And you could stand to get out a bit, too," Miles said.

"I know you of all people didn't just say that to me," Isaac said with a laugh.

After Miles's wife had left, Miles had devoted his entire life to caring for his son, never leaving his side. It took numerous conversations with every member of the family to convince Miles that Benji needed friends his own age and that Miles needed more in his life than his son. Finally, Miles had relented and joined the playgroup. Not only had he and Benji become regulars, most importantly, Miles had begun to give Benji more space. As a result, Benji had become independent and was making new friends. And Miles had reconnected with Jillian.

"Hard to believe, but it's true. Learn from my mistakes. Don't isolate yourself. You and Mia both need more than family in your lives. Make space for friends. Including a lady friend if one—emphasis on *one*—catches your eye."

Isaac instantly thought of his neighbor. He'd definitely be interested in creating some space for her.

"Are you coming back home?" Miles asked.

Isaac shook his head. Although he had returned to work, he had taken the morning off to spend time with Mia. Ranching was a seven-day-a-week enterprise, so if he took off a few hours on a weekday, there was still plenty of work to do on the weekends. "It's a nice day, so I'm going to walk around town for a bit. I think Mia will enjoy seeing the sights."

"See you later," Miles said and Jillian waved.

"Are you ready for an adventure?" Isaac asked as he put Mia into her stroller and then buckled her in. She kicked her legs, impatient to get the stroller moving. "All righty, then. Let's get this show on the road."

Savannah drove down the highway to town, determined to finish her shopping now. She could make do without most things, but she had no bacon, which constituted an emergency.

She'd tried to eat a bowl of cold cereal and toast, but she'd been left unsatisfied, so she was on her way to Aspen Creek on this bright Tuesday morning, hoping that the store wouldn't be too crowded. As she took the exit ramp, a dog ran in front of her car. She slammed on the brakes, thankful there wasn't anyone behind her as a bad crash could have resulted.

The dog trotted to the side of the road and sat down. Without giving it a second thought, Savannah pulled onto the shoulder and got out of her car. Slowly, cautiously, she approached the dog. He gave her a long look. If it had growled or looked threatening, she would have gotten back into her car. Instead, it whimpered softly.

"Are you doing this?" she asked herself. As her feet continued to move toward the animal, she replied to herself. "I guess I am."

When she was about foot away, she held out her hand for the dog to sniff. He did and then licked her fingers. "I suppose this means we're friends now."

The dog cocked its head and looked at her.

"Are you okay? Let me check." She did a quick once-over, although she wasn't sure what she was looking for. The dog didn't appear to have any outward injuries and it wasn't bleeding. Nor was he wearing a collar or tags. But his coat was clean and he appeared to have been in good health. Was he lost? Or had he been abandoned? It was a terrible thought, but she knew there were people cruel enough to leave a once-loved family pet on the side of the road to fend for itself.

"Well, what are we going to do?" Savannah asked, placing her hands on her hips. She certainly couldn't leave the dog there. "Bark if you have a suggestion."

The dog barked twice. Savannah blinked and stared. The dog seemed to be smiling at her.

"I guess I'm going to have to get you into my car."

The dog barked again and stood up. That was easy enough.

"Come on, then." She started to walk. The dog just stood there. Savannah had never owned a dog, so she didn't know if there was a magic word or signal that would make the dog come. She patted her thigh nervously as she waited for inspiration to strike. The dog instantly walked over to her. It took a moment for her to realize that tapping her leg had made the dog come. "Well, I'll be."

Savannah and the dog made it to the car and she let it in the front seat. Once she was behind the wheel, she rolled down the passenger window so the dog could stick its head out if he wanted to. She didn't know if that was the proper thing to do, but since she'd seen other drivers do it, she imagined it was something dogs liked.

Now that she was suddenly the custodian of a dog, Savannah's plan for the day changed. She couldn't take the animal into the store, and she didn't want to leave it in her car alone while she shopped. Besides, it was clear that the dog had been trained by someone and might be lost. For all she knew, some child was standing on his porch calling for his dog as tears slid down his cheeks. She couldn't let that child suffer just so she could grab a pound of bacon. Savannah had walked just about every street of Aspen Creek, so she knew where the veterinarian was located.

Driving the scenic streets with the dog beside her, she was once more impressed by just how idyllic the town appeared. Aspen Creek was like something out of a movie. The streets were pristine and there were several benches on each side. Overflowing flowerpots hung from the light posts while urns filled with green plants decorated every corner. The cobblestone sidewalks were a nod to the past. It was the town's overall tranquility that had drawn Savannah. Nothing about the place appeared real, which helped her to avoid *her* reality.

The angled parking spots in front of the veterinarian's office filled, she drove to the end of the block and parked in the library lot. As she got out, she noticed a man pushing a baby in a stroller. The dog barked and the man looked over at them. Savannah didn't have a leash, so she removed the belt from her jacket and looped it around the dog's neck, just to be on the safe side.

"Hi," the man called as he pushed the stroller in her direction. Shivers danced down her spine as she recognized that voice. Isaac. He'd purchased her groceries and dropped them off at the cabin. *And he bought me chocolate too.*

At first, she'd wondered how he'd known where she lived, but then she'd recalled that he'd mentioned he'd seen her around the ranch. He must be one of the Montgomery sons. When she'd first come to town, a woman had dropped by with a cake and introduced herself as Michelle Montgomery. She'd told Savannah that she had three sons who would help her if she needed anything. All she had to do was ask. Of course, she hadn't. She'd come here to find peace in the isolation, not join a community. She hadn't found lasting peace. At least, not yet. And it looked as if the community was trying to rope her in.

"Hi," she called back, hoping he would go on his way and not try to draw her into a conversation. She wanted to be alone, but she couldn't ignore him either. She wouldn't repay his kindness with rudeness.

"I'm not sure that you remember, but we met in the store. I'm Isaac Montgomery."

She nodded. He was one of the Montgomery sons, just as she'd suspected. "I remember. I'm Savannah Rogers."

"Nice to meet you, Savannah. This is Mia. Is it okay if we walk with you?"

She couldn't think of a way to say no that didn't sound unpleasant. And she wasn't going far. Truth be told, she wasn't sure she *wanted* to say no. "Yes. That's fine."

"Is your dog friendly?" he asked, stopping at a safe distance.

"He seems to be."

"What does that mean?" His brow wrinkled, but it didn't detract from his good looks. He was just as attractive as he'd been the other night. But there was more to him than his outward appearance. He'd already showed that he was thoughtful. More than that, he had an unknown something that appealed to her on an elemental level. She didn't like the feeling. The only thing for her to do was to resist it. Resist *him*.

"It's not really my dog. I found it on the side of the road. I'm going to take it to the vet so he can check for a chip."

"That's a nice thing to do."

"Speaking of nice, thanks for my groceries. And the chocolate. How much do I owe you?"

He waved a dismissive hand. "It wasn't that much. Consider it a belated housewarming gift."

"If you say so."

"I do. Ready?"

"As much as I'll ever be." She held tight to the

belt, but it proved to be unnecessary. The dog walked beside her calmly, increasing her belief that it had been someone's pet.

As they walked down the sidewalk, a sense of calm suffused her. When they reached the vet's office, Isaac held the door and Savannah stepped inside. To her surprise, Isaac pushed the stroller inside and stepped in behind her.

Empty chairs were lined up against two walls. A large scale was in front of a counter on the back wall. Two doors were open to empty examination rooms.

"Welcome," a smiling young woman said. "I'm Claire. How can I help you?"

Savannah led the dog to the counter. When she stopped, he sat down. "I found this dog today. I was hoping that you could check for a chip."

"Of course." She grabbed a scanner and ran it over the dog's back and then returned to the desk. Claire clicked on the computer and then looked back at Savannah. "Just what I thought."

"What?"

"This is Scout. He was Harvey Ratcliffe's dog."

"Who is that?"

"Mr. Ratcliffe lived in a house on the outskirts of town near the highway. He passed a few weeks ago. His nephew was cleaning out the house to put it on the market. I thought he was going to take Scout back home with him when he left town a few days ago." She frowned. "I guess not."

"Do you have a number for him so I can check?"

"No. I'm sorry. I have no way of reaching him."

Savannah blew out a breath. "Now what?"

"What do you mean?"

"Did this Mr. Ratcliffe have any other family?"

"No. He was a widower. He actually got Scout two years ago to keep him company."

"So what's going to happen to Scout?"

"He'll have to go to a shelter. Hopefully, he'll be adopted."

"Of course, Scout is two years old, and most people want puppies, so he might not be adopted," Isaac said. He looked pointedly at Savannah, raising one eyebrow.

"Is that true?" Savannah asked.

"Sadly, yes," Claire replied.

"If Scout isn't adopted, what will happen to him?"

"He'll live the rest of his life in the shelter."

Savannah sucked in a breath. She didn't want that to happen. Scout looked at her, his big brown eyes pleading. "What if I want him? What do I have to do?"

"Since he's abandoned, you just have to take him home. We have his medical records on file, and his vaccines are up-to-date. I'll see if the vet can check him over, just to be sure that he didn't sustain any injuries while he was wandering on his own. But he should be good to go."

Savannah paused. Was she really going to do this? She didn't know the first thing about dogs. But the idea of Scout possibly spending the rest of his life without a family was not something she was willing to risk. She was a smart woman. She could get a book about dogs.

Claire took a leash from a hook, put it on Scout, undid the belt and handed it to Savannah. "Have a seat. This shouldn't take long."

Savannah watched as Claire and Scout vanished down a corridor.

"You're doing a good thing," Isaac said.

Savannah heard the admiration in his voice and wondered why his approval made her feel all warm and tingly. "Scout has already lost so much. I can't let him lose more." It was ridiculous to relate to a dog like this, but she did. She and Scout had each lost their families. They were alone in the world. Perhaps they could help each other. It would be good to have something to keep her busy. Something to love. Loving a dog would be much safer than loving a man or a child.

Although one of the selling points of the cabin had been the solitude it provided, lately she had suffered through occasional bouts of loneliness. A dog would be good company.

Claire returned with Scout and the vet whom she introduced as Dr. Trevor Hunt.

"How is he?" Savannah asked.

"He's in perfect health. He was a little bit hungry, so I fed him and gave him some water." He glanced at the belt she'd been using as a leash. "We have plenty of leashes, so you can keep that one."

"Thank you."

"You're giving him a good home, so it's the least we can do."

"Does he need any additional shots since he was a stray for a while?"

"No. If you're sure about adopting Scout, we'll register you as his owner. Simply give your information to Claire."

Savannah took a deep breath. This was her last chance to back out. She wouldn't. Taking in this homeless dog felt right. "I'm sure. I want to adopt him."

"Wonderful. We'll get you all set up."

As Savannah followed the woman to the counter to handle the paperwork, she couldn't keep from glancing over at Isaac. He was grinning from ear to ear, and she couldn't help smiling in return. She felt a spark and her stomach tumbled and she realized that Isaac was awakening something deep inside her.

Whether she wanted him to or not.

Chapter Three

"Congratulations on becoming a dog owner," Isaac said as he held the door for Savannah. He hadn't intended to stay with her as she completed the paperwork, but she'd looked so shell-shocked it would have been wrong to leave her alone. He didn't know Dr. Hunt personally, only by reputation. He was a good, honest man, so Savannah would have been in good hands with him. But Isaac had a feeling that Savannah had needed a little moral support. Of course, judging from the way she kept her distance and rarely looked him in the eyes, that could be wishful thinking.

"Thanks. It's definitely not something that I was planning on doing today. Or any other day, for that matter. But it feels right." She smiled hesitantly.

"Dogs are great."

"Do you have one?"

"I don't personally have a dog at the moment. But I grew up with dogs. Some of them were pets, but others were strictly working dogs. At least, that was the plan. Somehow or another they all ended up working dogs slash pets. They still do."

"What do you mean 'working dogs'?"

"I'm a cattle rancher and we use dogs to help with the herding. In fact, we're neighbors. Our ranch and the ranch where you live share a property line."

"I met your mother when I first moved in. She was nice."

"She still is," he joked. "And let me guess. She volunteered the services of her sons."

Savannah laughed. It was a soft, sweet sound that did a number on Isaac's insides. He tried to resist, but there was something very appealing about Savannah. Perhaps it was the way that she seemed to be surprised by her own reaction to him. As if she wanted to keep him at arm's length, but was unable to do so.

He knew the feeling. Walking beside her down the street as if he didn't have a care in the world, he felt different. Vulnerable. As if he were being swept away by some force stronger than he was. He didn't like feeling out of control, but he wasn't going to try stop it. He was enjoying the sensations sailing through him too much. For the time being, he would go with the flow.

"Yes. Luckily, I didn't have to impose."

"It wouldn't have been an imposition. Neighbors help each other. If you ever need anything, just let me know."

She nodded, but he sensed a hesitation there. Reaching out was the last thing she would do.

For a moment, he wondered if his reputation had preceded him. Everyone knew he enjoyed the company of women, and they enjoyed his. Sure, his dating habits had more or less come to a halt since he'd returned home with Mia, but that hadn't changed the way he viewed dating. And his unwillingness to be in a committed relationship didn't make him unreliable. He was just as good a man as his more serious brothers. But maybe that wasn't what held her back.

They reached the pet store and she stopped. "I suppose I should get some dog food."

She didn't sound particularly enthused at the prospect. In fact, he heard a bit of dread in her voice. "A few chew toys and treats wouldn't hurt."

Her eyes widened and he suspected that she was on the verge of becoming overwhelmed. "What kind?"

Just as he thought. The enormity of the job she'd taken on was now hitting her. Since she'd helped him the other night, he would return the favor. "How about I go with you?"

"If you have the time."

"I do."

He opened the door, and they stepped inside. There were several people shopping with their leashed dogs. Savannah inhaled audibly and took a step closer to him. "Oh."

"Unless they've changed things, dog food and supplies are to the right."

"Okay." She grabbed a cart, squared her shoulders as if going to battle and then started toward the right.

He grabbed two chew toys and held them up. "These are really durable. And you can put peanut butter or treats inside."

"Peanut butter? Like the kind people eat?"

"Yes. It's safe for dogs as long as it doesn't contain Xylitol. So is cheese by the way."

She took them from him and dropped them into her cart. He examined a couple more and offered them to her. She nodded and he set them beside the others.

He picked up a rope. "Dogs like to play with these. You hold one end and let him pull on the other."

"Okay. I'll get it."

"That should be a good start. See which toys he likes best and go from there. Of course, he might prefer sticks. Or house shoes."

She frowned. "Are you kidding?"

"Partly."

She stared at Scout. "Do not chew my shoes. Okay?"

Scout barked once.

"That sounds like a yes to me," Isaac said.

"Me too."

They stepped into the treat aisle and Savannah instantly grabbed a pack. "What do you think of these bacon flavored treats?"

"I've never eaten them myself," Isaac said.

Savannah shook her head and laughed. "I meant for Scout."

He shrugged. "I don't see how you can go wrong with the king of breakfast food."

"My thoughts exactly." She added a couple of large bags to her cart, and they headed for the food aisle. "There are so many to choose from. Thank goodness Dr. Hunt recommended a brand. Otherwise I might not be able to make up my mind."

She reached for the sixty-pound bag.

"I'll get it," Isaac said, stepping around her. In a moment, he'd hefted the bag and put it onto his shoulder.

"Thanks."

"No worries."

Check out was quick and before long they were standing outside the store.

"Well, I guess I should head back to my car. I need to drop Scout off at home and then go shopping. I don't think it would be right to leave him in the car after all he's been through."

"That's true. I always thought it was a bit cruel to leave dogs in the car for any length of time."

Although Isaac had intended to show Mia more of the town, he turned the stroller toward the library parking lot. The days were getting warmer and longer, so there would be plenty of time to familiarize Mia with Aspen Creek. And since she was still a baby, he doubted that she cared that her trip had been cut short.

Savannah seemed more at ease as she walked beside him to the library parking lot. A soft breeze blew, lifting her hair from her neck and blowing a hint of her perfume in his direction. The floral scent suited her. Sweet and subtle. Even a bit remote. Her reticence appealed to him. Perhaps because of its rarity. Generally, women wanted to be with him.

He frowned. That wasn't entirely accurate. Women enjoyed his company because he showed them a good time. But none of the women had ever wanted to have a relationship with him. That worked because he hadn't been looking for a long-term relationship. He'd preferred to date in small doses. A night or two of fun, a week at the most, before they went their separate ways, smiles on their faces. Then it had been on to the next.

His life was different now—and not simply because he had Mia, who was depending on him. For the first time in his life, he was drawn to a woman who he wanted to spend a lot of time with. Not just a couple of days. He wasn't going to delude himself. He wasn't in love or anything remotely like that. But he was curious about her.

As they walked, Isaac's eyes swept over her body. She was trim yet shapely. Dressed in loose-fitting jeans, a pink-striped knit top and boots with sensible heels, she looked sexier than she should have.

When they reached her car, he loaded the dog food into her trunk while she put Scout into the rear passenger seat. Isaac held open her door for Savannah, waiting until she was behind the wheel before closing it. She turned on the engine and then lowered the window. "Thank you for all of your help. See you around."

He wanted something more definite than that, but before he could say anything, Mia let out a cry.

Savannah winced at the sound and then sped off. He wondered at her reaction, but didn't have time to give it much thought now.

"Okay, sweetie," Isaac said, giving his attention to Mia instead of the woman currently driving away from him. Now he had a name to go with the face. *Savannah*. The beautiful name suited her.

He picked up Mia and sang to her. When she calmed, he rummaged through the diaper bag and pulled out a bottle and a banana. One of the mom blog websites and a parenting book had suggested giving babies vegetables as snacks. He'd boiled spinach and smashed peas, but Mia had clamped her mouth shut, refusing to eat them. But she would eat a mashed banana.

Mia spotted the snack and she reached out. There was a bench in front of the library, so he sat there while he fed her, savoring the peaceful moment. He had never imagined that he would be a father at this age, but it was the best thing that had ever happened to him. He just wished it hadn't come at the cost of Lisa's life.

Isaac had no idea what he should tell Mia about her mother, but he knew he would need to tell her something. There had been very few photos of Lisa among her belongings. So, not wanting to run the risk that the movers would lose them, he'd packed them up and taken them on the plane with him. When he'd gotten home, he'd made duplicate copies of the pictures as well as the few he'd discovered on an old phone. He'd been mesmerized by the candid photos. Lisa had been as vibrant as she'd been reserved. Mia deserved to know that about her. She needed to know that Lisa had been loved.

Savannah was as reserved as Lisa had been. Beneath her reticence, he'd sensed deep grief. He wondered what she had lost.

Isaac shook his head, refusing to create a backstory for someone he barely knew. He wasn't a psychologist. His degree was in animal science with a minor in creative writing. But he was a student of human nature. He needed to be to know which woman would welcome a no-strings-attached good time and which would want to tie him up in knots.

Mia finished her snack and he laid her against his shoulder and patted her back. After a minute, she let out a most unladylike burp, and he laughed. Her head lolled against his shoulder and he gently lowered her and looked into her face. She was struggling to keep her eyes open. Naptime.

He crossed the parking lot and set her into her car seat before folding up the stroller and putting it into the SUV. Before he was out of the lot, Mia was snoring softly.

As Isaac drove home, his mind was filled with thoughts of Savannah. Although he'd spent a bit of time with her today, he didn't feel like he knew much more about her than he did that night at the big box store. In fact, he had even more questions and few answers.

What was her history? Why would a woman of her age move to such an isolated cabin? Isaac sighed. He didn't know the answers but planned to do everything in his power to find out.

Mia was still sleeping when he reached the ranch Friday morning, so he ever so gently lifted her from the car seat and carried her up the stairs to his parents' house. Isaac had tossed out the idea of hiring a daytime nanny, but Michelle had been offended at the notion. His mother babysat Benji and had welcomed having Mia around as well.

He had to admit that he preferred leaving Mia in his mother's care as opposed to that of a stranger. But he made sure not to take advantage. He worked as hard and fast as he could so that he could pick up Mia around dinnertime. And he never left Mia with Michelle on his off days.

"Is she asleep?" Michelle asked as Isaac stepped into the kitchen. Benji was in the adjoining family room, playing with his Matchbox cars. The television was on in the background, but neither Benji nor Michelle appeared to be paying much attention to it.

"Yes. She had a late night."

"Again?"

"Yeah." Isaac rubbed his jaw and yawned. "She's still waking up during the night, then staying awake until early morning."

"If you want, I can wake her up in an hour or so."

Isaac shook his head. If Mia wasn't sleeping well at night, it seemed cruel to wake her up during the day just to make his life easier. He would let her sleep when she wanted and deal with the fallout later.

"Her sleeping pattern is off," Michelle said. "Keeping her up in the afternoon won't hurt her. It will get her back on track."

"No. She got off track on her own. She'll get back on track that way too."

Michelle laughed and shook her head. Isaac knew his mother thought he was making a mistake, but that she respected his role as Mia's parent enough not to interfere. Heaven knew, he had enough doubts of his own and often wondered if Lisa had chosen him to raise Mia out of desperation. Every time he made a decision, he worried that it was the wrong one. Should he make her eat more when she turned her head away? Was she too hot in her undershirt? Too cold without it?

Isaac placed Mia in the crib his mother had insisted on buying, covered her with a thin blanket and then kissed her forehead. The depth of love he felt for this little baby staggered him. He hadn't known that it was possible to feel this strongly for another person—especially one he'd just met. Yet here he was, ready to walk through fire if that was what it took to keep her safe and give her the wonderful life she deserved.

After saying goodbye to his mother, Isaac texted Miles to find out where he was working and then got his horse from the stable. They were riding fence today and making repairs.

Isaac met him and they set out, talking as they went. Miles had always been the quieter of the three brothers, content with his own company. Then he'd fallen in love with his childhood friend, Jillian, who was a firecracker. She was exactly what Miles had needed to draw him out of his shell.

"How are wedding plans coming?" Isaac asked.

Miles laughed. "I have no idea and that's the way I like it. I told Jillian to let me know the time and place and I'll be there."

"And she let you get away with that?"

"Not at first. But when I suggested we have pigs in a blanket as an appetizer at the reception, she saw the wisdom in my way."

"But you don't even like—" Isaac laughed and shook his head. "They always say you need to watch out for you quiet types."

"*They* may be on to something. Seriously, I don't know the difference between one kind of table linen or another, or why a short centerpiece is better than a tall one. I mean, in the end, it doesn't matter to me. I just want Jillian to have her dream wedding down to the last detail. Whatever makes her happy makes me happy. I just can't wait to finally be married to her."

"That's not something I would want to do either."

"Not that you have to worry about it."

"What do you mean?"

"Come on, Isaac. You're not the marrying type. How is it you describe yourself? *Love 'em and leave 'em happy*? Not that there's anything wrong with it. That's the way you're made and there's no sense in pretending to be something that you're not."

That stung, although Isaac couldn't put his finger on why. Miles wasn't trying to hurt him. He was simply being honest. Before Mia had come into his life, he'd been a devoted partier. He'd changed, but nobody had seemed to notice. He hadn't been to a club in weeks. Surprisingly, he hadn't missed it all that much. True, he missed the company of women, but he wasn't longing to be with anyone in particular.

Instantly, a picture of Savannah popped into his mind and he realized that he had just lied to himself. He wanted to be with her.

They reached the boundary separating their ranch from the Duncan property and began checking the fence. They'd been riding for about twenty minutes when they spotted a hole. Jumping down from their horses, they grabbed their tools. Isaac heard barking a moment before a dog ran through the hole.

"Scout, come back here."

Isaac recognized Savannah's voice and his heart sped up. A moment later, her face appeared through the hole. Her caramel cheeks were tinged pink. Her hair was flying around her face and her breathing was coming in big gusts. Again, her unadorned beauty struck him; she was so different from the women he usually dated.

Scout ran in a wide circle, clearly ignoring Savannah's command.

Isaac let out a loud whistle. The dog froze and then sat down on his haunches. Isaac held out a hand and helped Savannah climb through the hole in the fence. He grinned at her. "How's the training going?"

She shot him a dirty look, which only made him smile broader. "We were inside for a while when I decided to let him explore the ranch. The past couple of days, I walked with him on the leash. He did really well. Today I took off the leash and let him run around on his own. That might have been a mistake."

He held up two fingers an inch apart. "Maybe a tiny one."

"He's still learning the boundaries. I'm sorry that he's on your property."

"No worries. We're fixing the hole in the fence, so he shouldn't be able to come over here as easily. Although, looking at him, I think he might be a bit of an escape artist. I won't be surprised if he finds his way over here occasionally even after we make the repairs."

He and Savannah looked at the dog who was sitting on the grass looking completely innocent.

"I didn't know he would be so fast. And adventurous. I think I bit off more than I can chew. I think he was on his best behavior at the vet because he wanted to fool me into taking him in."

"You think he was putting you on?"

"Maybe."

Isaac laughed. Then he sobered. "You aren't thinking about taking him to the shelter, are you?"

"No. He's a rascal, but he's my rascal. I already love him. I might need to take him to obedience school, though." She sounded less than enthused at the prospect.

"Maybe not. He'll probably settle down soon. Remember, he lived in a house with an old man before and probably didn't get to run around a lot. Now he has acres and acres of land. He's just enjoying his freedom."

"Spoken like an expert."

"I told you that we had dogs growing up, so if you need help, just holler. Let me give you my cell number in case you have questions."

Savannah gave him an unreadable look and he wondered if he was coming on too strong, something he'd never worried about before. But then, he'd never dated anyone as reticent as Savannah.

"Okay. That sounds good."

"If you want, you can give me your number and I'll call your phone, so you'll have my number."

Savannah hesitated for a moment then held out her hand for his phone. She typed in her number and then listened. After a moment, she smiled. "Now we have each other's numbers, although I can't imagine you'll need to call me for help."

In other words, Don't call me.

He heard a chuckle and looked over where Miles

was standing. Apparently, his brother was getting a kick out of watching Isaac be shot down. "Let me introduce you to my brother Miles."

Miles stepped over to them, his hand extended. "Hi, I'm Miles, Isaac's older brother."

"Savannah Rogers." She smiled as she shook his hand.

"It's nice to meet you, Savannah."

"Same." She looked over at Scout, who was now sniffing the grass. "I guess I should get my dog so you can get back to what you were doing." Her brow wrinkled. "What are you doing?"

"We're repairing the fence. We have a lot of cattle and don't want them getting off of our property. They generally don't graze this far out, so don't worry about seeing a cow on your deck."

She nodded. "That's good to know. I'm not sure I'm ready for a dog, but I know I'm not ready for a cow. Speaking of… Scout. Come."

The dog gave her a *You're not the boss of me* look and continued sniffing the ground.

"Scout. Come," Isaac said.

The dog ran over to them. When he reached Savannah, he wagged his tail and then sat down. Savannah shook her head, clearly aggravated, and then turned and began walking away. After a moment, the dog followed.

"Do you ride horses?" Isaac called to her retreating back. He wasn't ready to let her go just yet.

"No."

"Would you like to go riding some time? I can teach you how. It's not hard. Then I can show you the ranch."

She frowned and his heart stopped beating as he awaited her answer. "I don't know."

"It'll be fun," he coaxed. "If you're going to live in ranch country, it wouldn't hurt to get comfortable around horses."

"Is that right?"

He nodded. "We have some smaller horses. Gentle horses that you will love riding."

"That sounds like it would be okay." She paused, as if debating, and he held his breath. Finally, she spoke. "Yes. I guess I'll go riding with you."

Isaac smiled. "I'll call you."

She nodded and then hurried away.

Isaac watched as Savannah and Scout went back through the hole in the fence. Anticipation and happiness filled him. He had a date with Savannah.

He felt a shove and glanced at Miles, who was smirking. "I never thought I'd see the day."

"What day is that?"

"The day you have to beg a woman to go out with you."

Isaac shook his head. "I wasn't begging."

"Think not? I half expected you to break out the knee pads."

"Now I know you've lost your mind. That was simply me asking a woman to go horseback riding."

"A woman who was walking away from you."

Trust Miles to point that out. Isaac sighed. "I admit that I'm attracted to Savannah and would like to get to know her better, okay?"

"And?"

"I don't know. There's something there I can't name." He wasn't sure he wanted to. "Let's get back to work. I don't want to be late getting Mia."

Miles nodded and mercifully let the subject drop. As they worked, Isaac couldn't help wondering why he was so determined to get to know Savannah when he wasn't sure she was quite as interested.

"You and I are going to have to talk about boundaries," Savannah said, pointing her finger in Scout's face. She could swear the dog was grinning at her. Ignoring that ridiculous notion, she soldiered on. "I need you to stay in our yard. You have enough space to run and play, so there's no reason for you to venture over to the Montgomery ranch."

Scout barked once and then lay his head on his front paws, doing his best to look adorable. She sighed. "See, this was why I've never had a dog. You play your humans. Try to act all innocent when you're guilty as heck."

If she didn't know better, she'd think that Scout had intentionally sought out Isaac. But she did know better. The dog was just doing what dogs did. Get into trouble.

She had to admit that Isaac had looked incredible. Dressed in faded jeans, plaid shirt, cowboy boots and hat, he looked like a rancher from central casting. He'd been dressed similarly each time she'd seen him, so she didn't know why he'd made such an impression on her today. Perhaps it was the horse. After she'd gotten Scout on their side of the fence, she'd stood behind a bush that shielded her from Isaac's sight, all the while allowing her to watch him. When he and his brother had finished repairing the fence, they'd gotten on their horses and ridden away.

Something about the way Isaac had swung himself onto the back of that majestic animal had made her mouth water. He'd looked so strong. So masculine. As if nothing in the world could hurt him.

The shocking thought took her breath away and brought her back to reality. No man was impervious to danger or death—no matter how strong and muscular. Nobody was invincible. Harm came to everyone eventually and she couldn't endure the pain of losing another person. She had barely survived losing Darren and Tony. Sometimes she wondered if she had survived. Even after all this time, the ache was still there. The pain wasn't as debilitating as it had been, but it was still her constant companion. A reminder of what it felt like to lose the most important people in her life. A warning to keep her distance and not make the mistake of loving ever again.

And so far she had. She'd moved from the city with its constant reminders of her lost husband and child. She could walk down the main thoroughfare of Aspen Creek without passing a store where Darren had bought his favorite suits. She didn't have to worry about being assaulted by memories of Tony being mesmerized by colorful Christmas lights dangling from streetlights. Darren and Tony had never stepped foot in Aspen Creek, so there were no memories to make her weep at unexpected times.

So why, knowing how much she would risk by becoming involved with Isaac, was she still thinking about him? Why was she yearning for his company? Fear alone should have her building barbed-wire fences around her heart.

"Because you're a glutton for punishment," she muttered to herself as she walked back to the cabin.

Scout barked in agreement and ran and got the ball, dropping it at her feet so they could play fetch. After an endless game that Savannah hoped wore him out, she brought the dog back inside.

Her phone pinged and she checked the text. Cheyenne, her older sister, doing her bi-weekly check in.

How are things?

Savannah typed back her usual Fine. With you?

All's well in the kingdom.

There was a long pause and Savannah knew her sister was waiting—hoping for more. They'd always been close, sharing secrets. After five minutes, her phone pinged again.

Take care, Savannah. I love you. Ttyl.

Savannah stared at the phone for a moment and then typed.

I got a dog.

You? I don't believe it.

Neither do I.

But then, I guess I can see you with a tiny poodle or some other teacup dog.

Savannah turned the camera phone toward Scout, who immediately sat up and posed. What a ham. Savannah sent the copy of the picture to her sister, and a smile tugging on the edges of her lips, waited for Cheyenne's response.

Whoa. That dog is huge. LOL.

Tell me about it. He's a black lab. Scout was a stray in need of a home. I couldn't let him go to a shelter.

Good for you. You always had a heart built for love.

Did she? Maybe. But she wasn't willing to love again. It hurt too much when loved ones were snatched away.

I've got to go now. For real this time. Ttyl.

Ttyl.

Savannah felt much lighter after she ended the call.

Although she'd intended to complete her shopping the day she'd adopted Scout, she hadn't had the heart to leave the dog alone in a strange place. Not only that, she'd maxed out on people. Now Scout had made himself at home, and he hadn't shown a desire to chew her shoes, so she felt comfortable leaving him alone for a while. She gave Scout his favorite chew toy and then closed her bedroom door. She filled his water bowl and then left, hoping that he wouldn't destroy the house in her absence.

The big box store wasn't crowded and she was able to gather her groceries easily. She had just paid for everything when she heard her name being called.

No way. She turned and watched as Isaac walked toward her, a bag in one hand. What was he doing here?

"I thought that was you," he said.

"I needed to finish shopping."

"Me too. I forgot to get diapers when I was here before. My mother is watching Mia for me, so I could make this quick trip."

She nodded. So where was Mia's mother?

"You want to grab a cup of coffee in the café before we head back?"

Everything inside her told her to say no. That would be the rational thing to do. The safe thing to do. Yet the way he'd phrased it, saying *before we head back*, made her feel less alone. "I suppose that would be all right."

"Great." He took her cart, steered it toward the food area, and then looked at her, his ever-present smile on his face. "What would you like?"

"Coffee?"

"Anything else? A muffin? Bag of chips? Hot dog?"

"That sounds like a trick question."

"How so?"

"Like you want something more, but you think it'll be rude to eat if I don't."

"Well, it would be, but that's not why I asked."

"In that case, I wouldn't mind a hot dog and some chips. And I guess I'll exchange the coffee for a large lemonade."

"That sounds perfect. I'll have the same."

Isaac gave their order to the concession worker, who stopped flipping through a magazine long enough to ring it up, and then pulled out his wallet.

"I should get this," Savannah said. She slid her debit card into the card reader before he could object.

"Why? I invited you."

"Maybe. But you paid for my groceries the other night. I owe you."

"I told you before, you don't owe me a thing. We're neighbors. And I would like to be friends."

Friends. She tried the word on for size. It didn't fit too badly, so she nodded. "I guess that would be okay."

She couldn't be certain, but it looked like relief flashed on his face before he smiled. That was ridiculous. Her friendship couldn't matter that much to him.

They found a clean table, sat down and doctored their hot dogs with mustard, relish and onions. She opened her chips and took out one. It hit her that this was the first time she'd eaten with anyone in months. At least, voluntarily. There had been the repast after the funeral, but she hadn't been able to choke down more than a forkful of spaghetti. She'd sipped fruit punch and waited for the moment when she could escape the other mourners and return to a house that was no longer a home. A house that was too big. Too silent. Too empty. It hadn't provided the refuge she'd sought.

She'd tried working, but being around the other faculty and her students hadn't felt right. It had been too hard to pretend that she wasn't dying inside. Her dean had expressed disappointment but not surprise when she'd told him she was taking a sabbatical.

Her parents had invited her to stay with them in North Carolina, where they had retired after her father had given up his practice as a cardiologist.

Her brother had wanted her to move to New York and stay with him and his family. Only her sister had understood her need to be alone in a new place.

She chased the thoughts away before they could ruin her appetite.

Savannah was suddenly curious about Isaac. She wouldn't ask him anything personal since she had no intention of answering personal questions. Before she could get out the first question, he opened up. Clearly, he wasn't nearly as reserved as she was.

"This is the first time I've been out without Mia in…well…since I got her."

"What do you mean *got her*?"

He laughed ruefully. "I guess that was a pretty strange way of putting things. Mia has only been with me for a little over a month. Since February, actually."

"So, you aren't divorced?"

"No. I've never been married."

She nodded. He'd piqued her curiosity and she took a swallow of her lemonade to keep from peppering him with questions she didn't want turned back on her.

"I'm going to trust you with something only my family knows. That is, if it's okay with you?"

"Why wouldn't it be?"

"Not everyone wants to be burdened with a secret."

"You didn't kidnap her, did you?" She was only half joking.

He laughed. The sexy sound made her stomach

somersault. "No. You really are funny. I didn't expect that."

"Why not?"

"I don't know." He hesitated. "There's a somberness to you. Something I can't put my finger on."

He was partly right. Once, she'd been the life of the party. The person always up for a good time. She'd been the one who'd arranged all of the girls' nights out with her friends. The one who'd discovered new restaurants to try, or insisted that she and Darren host game nights at their house. But that was in the before times. She couldn't imagine wanting to socialize with anyone again—even her old friends.

She shrugged. "You could be right. But what is the secret? I won't tell anyone. Ever." Considering the fact that she hadn't had a real conversation with anyone other than Isaac since Darren and Tony had been taken from her, that would be an easy promise to keep. Sure, she talked with her parents once a month or so, but they wouldn't care about some stranger's secret.

"Mia is my daughter in all the ways that count, but she's not my biological child. Her mother was a friend of mine who died of cancer. She wanted me to raise Mia."

"What about the father?"

"She said he was out of the picture."

"That could mean anything."

"I know. But there was no indication that he was

ever in Mia's life or had any interest in becoming involved."

"That sounds like he's out of the picture."

Isaac nodded. "I've had my ups and downs with this new dad thing—I can't get her to keep on socks to save my life—but I can't imagine my life without her."

Savannah pictured the cute little girl and her heart seized. Mia had lost her mother so young and would never have any memories of being held in her loving arms. From the little she'd seen of Isaac, he was doing his best to be a good father. The two seemed happy together. And Savannah had enjoyed the little time she'd been with them.

What would it be like to spend more time with them? Would she be happy? Would the huge hole in her heart shrink? Would her loneliness diminish? What kind of thinking was that?

She shook her head. What was she doing here with Isaac? They couldn't be friends. If something happened to Mia, he would be devastated. If she let them get any closer, she would be too. Just listening to how Mia came to be with him drove home the point that nobody's life was without pain. Savannah stood. "I'm sorry. I can't do this."

Isaac had been about to eat a chip. His hand was now suspended between the table and his mouth. He stood, dropping his hand to the table. She didn't think he noticed the chip falling to the ground. "I don't understand. Can't do what? Keep the secret?"

"No. Yes. Of course, I'll keep it. Your story isn't mine to tell."

"Then what can't you do?"

"I can't do this." She waved a hand between them. "I can't do us."

"Us? I'm offering friendship. That's all. Can you do that?"

She wanted to. Being his friend sounded nice. He was considerate and witty. Although she didn't want to admit it to herself, and would certainly never admit it to him, she was attracted to him. Not just physically, though he was a handsome man. She was attracted to his character. It would be easy to get used to having him around. So easy to fall for him. And that wasn't a risk she was willing to take. "No. I'm sorry, Isaac. I can't."

She took a step away from him and tripped over her chair. She would have fallen if he hadn't grabbed her arm and then steadied her on her feet. "You don't have to run. I won't chase you. And I won't try to convince you to stay. Okay?"

Savannah nodded. She was making a fool of herself, but she couldn't help it. She had to get away before she did what she really wanted to do—accept the friendship he was offering.

And, more importantly, that she longed to accept.

Chapter Four

Isaac dropped back into the chair and tried to figure out what had gone wrong. The surprise he'd felt at running into Savannah had dulled somewhat. Seeing her twice in one day was a treat he hadn't expected. But he definitely hadn't anticipated her admitting that she wouldn't—okay, couldn't, in her words—even accept his friendship.

He was confused. Truly. He wanted to understand...but for the first time, Isaac found himself unsure of what to do around a woman he felt drawn to. Because he did know one thing—yeah, he was attracted to Savannah, but there was something more to it. He ached to figure out what it was, but how could he do that if he was never around her? He'd been glad to have a little time with Savannah, had hoped that sharing a small bite together would give him a chance to get to know her a little better. Hell, he wanted as much time with Savannah as he could get. Besides, he'd noticed her clothes were a tiny bit loose on her. As if she'd lost weight. He didn't think she was strapped for cash, but you never knew what people were going through.

Or perhaps she'd been sick, and maybe she was staying at the cabin while she recovered? That could explain her somberness. But that notion didn't quite fit. She might be a little thin, but she still had a pretty healthy appearance. Frowning, he stopped trying to figure it out. He could come up with a dozen different scenarios and each one of them could be wrong. Even if he hit upon the right one, it wouldn't explain why she kept running away from him.

He gathered the remains of their snack and tossed them into the garbage. Then he grabbed the diapers, hopped into his SUV and went home. When he stepped inside his parents' living room, Mia was wide-awake and "talking" to her grandfather.

Edward smiled at Isaac. "This little one is going to be quite the charmer. She's already talked me into getting her a pony."

"You don't say."

Isaac and each of his brothers had learned to ride by sitting in front of their father while they were only a little bit older than Mia. He didn't remember, of course, but framed photographs of them riding with Edward were scattered around the house. They didn't get their own horse until they were in middle school and could prove that they were responsible enough to care for it. Apparently, that rule wasn't going to apply to Mia.

"I do say."

"And who is going to feed and groom this horse? Who is going to clean the stall?"

"She's assured me that she knows a guy."

Isaac laughed and Mia turned to reach for him. "Dadada?"

"That's right. Your dada is here." He took her from his father's arms and gave her a big kiss on her cheek. She flashed him a four-tooth grin. "I suppose I'm the guy you told grandpa about."

"Exactly," Edward added.

"Well, Ms. Mia, it sounds like you're getting a pony."

Mia tossed her head and laughed.

"I guess I'd better get this little one home," Isaac said. He looked around. "Where's Mom?"

"Upstairs. She wanted me to remind you that Mia slept all day and that you can expect to be up all night."

Isaac sighed. "Did she have an I-told-you-so look on her face?"

"You already know." Edward stood. "And on that note, I'm going to bed. See you tomorrow."

"Tomorrow," Isaac repeated.

Edward chucked Mia under her chin, making her giggle, and then headed upstairs.

"Hey, Dad," Isaac called.

Edward looked over his shoulder. "Yes?"

Isaac's voice grew thick. He wasn't one given for broadcasting his feelings, but Lisa's death had made him realize that someone you loved can be snatched away from you without warning. He didn't want to leave anything left unsaid. "I just wanted to let you know I appreciate all that you've done for me all of my life. You've been a really great father and…and I love you."

Edward nodded. "I've always known you appreciated me. But it's good to hear. And I love you, too."

Isaac smiled as he left. His house wasn't far from his parents' place, so he and Mia were home in minutes. Mia might be wide-awake, but he knew she would eventually nod off, so he changed her into a nightgown and put on sleep pants of his own. He had never been a fan of pajamas, but now that he had a child in the house, he couldn't sleep in the nude any longer. He'd tried sleeping in a top, but it was too hot. Besides, the bottoms were confining enough.

Once dressed, he continued the nightly ritual he was trying to establish—reading. He wanted Mia to appreciate all kinds of literature and exposed her to a variety of authors. Tonight he'd started with Jack Prelutsky. When he'd read the last word, she was still wide-awake, so he picked up a book by Francisco X. Alarcón. Nikki Giovanni, and Shel Silverstein soon followed. Mia wasn't showing any signs of sleepiness, but his eyes were getting heavy. His cell phone rang, keeping him from drifting off.

"Yep?" he answered without checking the screen.

There was a long pause. Wrong number? He was about to check the caller ID when a tentative voice came over the phone. "Isaac?"

"Savannah?"

"Yes. It's me"

"Is everything okay?"

"Yes. And no."

"Do you need me to come over?" He jumped to his feet. "I can be there in five minutes."

"That's not necessary. I'm fine."

"Are you sure?"

"Yes."

"Okay." He eased back into his chair, his heart rate slowing back to normal.

She didn't say anything else, and he wondered if he should stop by anyway, just to be on the safe side.

Finally, she spoke in a low voice. "I want to apologize to you."

"For what?"

"For running away from you. Again. That was rude."

"You don't need to apologize to me. Not for that."

Another pause. Then, "Are you always like this?"

"Like what?"

"So...easygoing. So understanding."

"I hope so."

"Why?"

"Because life is hard enough without being a jerk."

She laughed. "That's one way of putting it."

"Seriously, you don't need to apologize. You felt like leaving, so you left. Simple as that."

"I feel like I owe you an explanation at the very least."

"You don't owe me that either. Savannah, I don't know what type of people you're used to dealing with, but I don't expect anything from you."

"Maybe I want to explain. Or at least to talk."

"You can talk about anything you want. I'll listen."

Another long pause came over the line. "I was married before."

"Okay."

"His name was Darren. He was...killed." Her voice trembled on the last word. She hesitated again. "In an accident."

"I'm so very sorry." That explained the somberness he sensed in her.

"We had a son. Tony. My baby's name was Tony... He was with Darren in the car when it was hit. He...he died too."

Isaac heard the tears in her voice and his throat ached, leaving him unable to speak for several long seconds. "That's terrible. Savannah, I'm so very, very sorry. I know those words don't do a thing to make you feel better, but I mean them."

"I know you do. And, no, they don't help. Nothing does."

"I don't want to start spewing meaningless platitudes, so I'll just be quiet and listen."

"There's nothing more to say. I just wanted to explain why I ran away." She sighed. "I guess I wasn't clear. I was devastated when they were taken from me. I think I heard every cliché at least once, so I appreciate that you didn't repeat them. I know people were trying to comfort me, but that was impossible. The two people I loved most in the world were gone forever. Words couldn't change that. Everyone spoke of time healing wounds, but it hasn't. I tried keeping busy, but that didn't ease the pain either. I miss them every day. Just as much as ever." Her voice was so anguished, he actually felt her pain.

It was hard for him to speak. But he knew he had to say something. "I imagine you always will miss them. Hopefully, the pain will diminish eventually, and you'll be able to remember happy times."

"That's what everyone says. But when I think of happy times, I just think of everything they missed. What we all missed, as a family."

"I can see how that would happen."

"And that's why I can't be your friend."

"Because your husband and son aren't here to be with their friends?"

"No. Because I can't run the risk of losing another person."

Now he understood. She'd suffered an unimaginable loss and she wasn't willing to risk enduring another one. "I get it."

"Especially someone with a baby. Just looking at Mia made me realize just how empty my arms are. I want to hold my sweet boy and kiss his chubby cheeks, but I'll never be able to do that again. I'll never hear him giggle and call me mommy."

"I'm sorry that being around us brings you pain. That's the last thing I ever want to do."

"I. Uh." She cleared her throat. "That's all I wanted. To explain, so that you could understand where I'm coming from." She grew quiet. "I guess… I'll just say goodbye, Isaac. And thank you, for everything."

He longed to keep her talking. To try to find a way to ease the pain he heard in her voice. But he could tell there was nothing he could say. "Good night, Savannah."

After the call ended, Isaac stared at his phone, still reeling from what he'd heard. That explained so much. He hated to think of what she'd suffered. Though he intended to honor her request, he wished he knew a way to ease her pain. She was a kind woman who deserved happiness.

Savannah expected to feel relieved after she'd told Isaac that they couldn't be friends, but the feeling had never come. Instead, she was filled with regret. For the past four hundred and forty-six days, she had been content to be on her own. Oh, she couldn't avoid the obligatory monthly check-in phone call with her parents or the semi-regular texts with her siblings, but other than that, she'd been able to limit her human interactions. And she'd been happy. Well, as happy as she could be without Darren and Tony.

Now she found herself experiencing something she hadn't felt in a long time. Longing for human company. And not just any human. She wanted to be with Isaac.

The whole idea terrified her. She didn't want to yearn for his company or to have this uncertain, wobbly feeling in her stomach whenever he was around. After living through the crippling pain following Darren and Tony's deaths, she'd managed to reach a state of blessed numbness. Ice had enveloped her heart, protecting her from feeling. She'd been so careful to keep people at a distance, to avoid any kind of relationships. She'd tried to keep Isaac at arm's length, but somehow he had managed to slip past her barriers. He had managed to reach a place inside her where she cared about him.

Simply thinking about him made her heart skip a beat. He'd looked so good yesterday while they'd had a hot dog together. A snack that had turned into her dinner. She'd been so stressed when she'd gotten home that she'd put away the groceries, taken Scout out to do his business, and then crawled into bed, trying to rid herself of the emotions churning inside her.

Not that she'd gotten much sleep. Every time she'd closed her eyes, she'd pictured Isaac's compassionate eyes as he'd told her about his friend's death. He was such a good man. He hadn't complained once about the upset that suddenly having a daughter must have caused him. He actually seemed thrilled to have Mia in his life.

He'd been so kind to her on the phone last night. Although she hadn't seen his face, she'd heard the concern in his voice. The compassion. While others had spoken what they'd intended to be words of comfort, he hadn't. Instead, he'd validated her feelings and admitted to not knowing what to say.

He had been one of the few people who'd actually acknowledged her grief without urging her to move past it. Hadn't told her that time healed all wounds. That she should begin to reenter society and rejoin her friends in activities she'd previously enjoyed. To fake it until she could make it.

Didn't they know she would love nothing more than to not have that knot of misery in her chest all of her waking hours? She might not be suffering as much now, but the hurt was there. Not having to explain that to Isaac had made him all the more appealing.

His conversation had felt like a comforting hug and a part of her wished that his arms had actually been around her. She could only imagine how heavenly it would be to have him hold her close. To be able to lean her head on his shoulder and breathe in his cologne. The thought had frightened her last night. It was less frightening in the light of day.

She called for Scout. It was a beautiful day and she wanted to be in it. After fastening his leash, she headed out the back door. When she'd moved here, the real estate agent had told her that she was free to roam the nearly one-hundred-acre property. She hadn't. To date, she'd only seen the inside of the cabin and the two acres of manicured lawn that surrounded it. And, of course, a bit of the Montgomery ranch. Landscapers maintained the lawn, so she hadn't even had to rake a leaf or mow the grass. Now she was curious about what secrets the woods behind her cabin held.

She tucked her cell phone into her pocket and set off on her adventure. Her natural curiosity was peeking out today and she had to admit she liked it.

"Which way should we go?" she asked Scout. The dog immediately pulled the leash in the direction of the Montgomery ranch, and she pulled him back. "Not today. We can't go over there today."

Her pulse raced at the thought of seeing Isaac again. But that was the opposite of staying away from him.

Savannah had never been wishy-washy. Once she made a decision, she stuck to it. She didn't give mixed signals. She didn't want Isaac to think that she was playing with his feelings. She'd told him straight-out that they couldn't be friends, so it would be unfair to seek him out the very next day.

Not that she knew where he was. His ranch was huge, and she didn't know if the border was straight or if it curved. Although she'd lived next to his ranch for over a year, she'd spent most of that time locked inside the cabin, trying to escape her pain. She'd only recently begun to explore her backyard.

What she knew about ranching couldn't fill a thimble. What did he do all day? She knew that he repaired fences, but only because she'd seen him and his brother doing it yesterday. Did he have to feed the cows? Milk them?

Why was she wondering about this now when she hadn't spared her neighbors a thought in the past? When she'd first moved to Aspen Creek, she hadn't known what type of ranchers her neighbors were. Hadn't cared. Back then, she'd been trying to get through one hour. One morning. One afternoon. One night. And then start all over again. Now she wanted to know more about her surroundings and her neighbors. Or, more accurately, one in particular.

How much of her curiosity was due to the length of time she'd lived here and how much was due to her exceptionally attractive and charming neighbor? She had no idea. That was a question for another time. A time when she would be able to think about him without her heart threatening to burst out of her chest. So…maybe…never?

She and Scout crossed the sunny backyard and stepped into the woods. The temperature dropped a little, but was still comfortable. The canopy of trees played peekaboo with the sun, creating a magical, dappled appearance all around her. She wouldn't be surprised to stumble across elves or fairies dancing in the meadow. One of Tony's favorite bedtime stories took place in a community of elves and fairies. He'd always laughed and pointed at a colorful picture of the mountain village they lived in.

She suddenly realized that the village in the picture bore a striking resemblance to Aspen Creek. Had that been the reason she'd settled here? Had her subconscious recognized the place and been looking for her son here?

The thought brought her up short and she tripped over a tree root, barely managing to regain her balance before she hit the ground. Her vision blurred and she blinked away the sudden tears. This little town and these woods would have enchanted Tony. She could picture him wandering around the trees and looking for fairies beside a babbling brook; claiming that the wild mushrooms were their houses so he and Savannah had to be very careful where they stepped.

She wished he was here now. He'd been such a

happy little boy, finding delight in everything. But he was gone, so she would look around in his stead and try to find the happiness on his behalf.

She and Scout trampled through the trees until they came upon a stream in a sunny meadow. She sat down on a boulder while Scout sniffed around. She lifted her face to the sun and closed her eyes. Inhaling deeply, she filled her lungs with fresh air, mingling with the scent of wildflowers. Birds chirped, filling the woods with their happy song.

After a while, Scout had sniffed everything he found worthy of a sniff, and he returned to her side. They wandered for about an hour longer before Savannah decided it was time to return to the cabin. She'd always believed she had a sense of direction, but suddenly she had no idea which way to go. Had they come from the right or the left? She considered using the compass on her phone, but then realized that it didn't matter which way was north since she had no idea which direction the cabin lay.

Putting her hands on her hips, she frowned and then picked a direction. "Let's go, Scout."

After about forty minutes, she realized that they weren't heading for the cabin. She was trying to come up with a plan when she heard a man's laughter. Goose bumps rose on her skin as she recognized Isaac's voice. Apparently, she was near the Montgomery property line.

Scout heard the laughter, barked, and then started

trotting toward his friend's voice, pulling Savannah with him. In minutes, she saw Isaac. Her heart skipped a beat as if ignoring the fact that she had decided they weren't going to be a part of each other's lives.

"Hey," Isaac said by way of greeting, slipping his cell phone into his shirt pocket.

Scout pulled against the leash, so Savannah released it. The dog ran over to Isaac's side, and Isaac knelt down and gave him a big rub.

"Hi." Savannah's heart thudded. She told herself that it had nothing to do with Isaac. That it was only relief at no longer being lost. She knew she was lying.

"I'm surprised to see you out this way."

"Scout and I decided to take a walk. I got twisted around and somehow ended up on your property."

"Is that right?" He stared at her from beneath his hat. She'd never been especially impressed by cowboys, but there was something about Isaac that challenged that old notion.

"Yes. So, if you'll give me directions back to the cabin, I'll get out of your hair."

"I can do you one better. I have my horse, so I'll give you a ride."

"What about Scout?"

"I don't think Samson will be all that thrilled about having a dog on his back."

She laughed and poked him in his chest. It felt

as hard as it looked. "That's not what I meant and you know it. I meant, will he be able to keep pace with a horse?"

"Sure. I'll be leading Samson and I won't walk too fast for Scout."

Everything inside her warned her to say no. To stick to her vow to keep him at a distance. "Yes. I would love that."

Smiling broadly, Isaac held out his hand and she took it. His skin was callused from the work he did, but his touch was gentle. Her fingers tingled dangerously at the contact.

He led her to the left side of the horse. "Put your left foot in this stirrup and then swing your right leg over and around."

"Okay." Savannah followed Isaac's instruction. When she was sitting on the horse, she looked down and realized just how high she was in the air. "Whoa."

"Don't panic," Isaac said.

The horse swayed and she grabbed onto the saddle. A squeak escaped her before she could fight it back. Maybe this wasn't the best idea. "That's easy for you to say. You're standing on the ground."

"You're perfectly safe. I promise."

She inhaled deeply. "Is your horse strong enough to hold us both?"

"Yes."

"Then maybe you should ride with me. That way you can catch me if I fall."

"If you're sure."

"Positive. Now hurry up."

"Okay." He swung up behind her. His arms encircled her as he grabbed the reins. She held herself stiffly, even though she really wanted to relax into his muscular torso. The thought was so shocking that she jerked to attention. She wouldn't be leaning against Isaac now. Or ever. In fact, she wasn't supposed to be letting him into her life. Yet here she was sitting in front of him on a horse.

"Relax. You'll enjoy the ride much better that way."

His voice was near her ear and she realized that he had leaned close to her. So close, if she turned her head, her lips would brush his. The thought made her shiver. She reminded herself that they didn't have that kind of relationship. They didn't have a relationship at all.

She closed her eyes. Who was she kidding? Despite her protestation, she and Isaac were building a relationship. They were definitely more than mere neighbors. If she gave even a little bit, they could become friends. Would that be so wrong?

"Are you afraid?"

She shook her head in answer to his question and to her own. "Nope. I'm fine."

"It will be a lot easier and more fun if you open your eyes. Unless you're able to see with your ears."

Despite herself, she laughed and opened her eyes. "You're not funny."

"Yes, I am."

Okay, maybe he was a bit funny. But he was too confident—too attractive—for her to admit it to him.

He gave the reins a little shake. "Let's go, Samson."

The horse took a step and its big body shifted. Startled, Savannah let out a little gasp and grabbed Isaac's wrists.

"Don't be afraid. I won't let you fall."

"I know. I just wasn't expecting it to feel this way."

"What way?"

"Like the earth is shifting beneath me." In more ways than one.

"You'll get used to it." He turned his head. "Scout. Come."

The dog looked up from the patch of grass he'd been sniffing, barked and began to walk beside the horse.

"Samson won't step on Scout, will he?"

"No. He's used to being around dogs. And believe it or not, Scout won't step in Samson's path. He has the same sense of self-preservation that you have."

Savannah relaxed. "I kind of like the view from up here. It's all so beautiful."

"I know. I don't like to brag but—"

"Yes, you do."

"Yes, I do what?"

"You like to brag, so admit it."

"I guess I do brag about the ranch. But I'd be lying if I didn't point out that it's the most beautiful piece of land in Colorado. No matter which direction you look, you see nature at its finest. We have green hills, beautiful lakes and flowing rivers. And, of course, the mountains in the distance. You can travel all over and you won't find anything to rival what we have here."

"I haven't seen much, but I am impressed."

"If you want, I can take you to see more of the ranch."

She nodded without thinking. Clearly, her sense of self-preservation was losing the battle to keep Isaac out of her life. But she did want to see more of the ranch.

"What's that?" she asked, pointing across the vast expanse of grass and trees to a small structure.

"That's a shelter for the cattle. For the most part, the cows live outside. We have a few shelters for them on the range to protect them in rough weather."

"That's a nice thing to do."

"Nice." He chuckled. "How much do you know about cattle ranching?"

"I know that cattle live outside and that ranchers build shelters for them. Oh, and that you have to fix fences."

He laughed. "In other words, nothing."

"My knowledge is limited to what you've told me. But I do want to know more."

"Well, if you decide you want to go riding with me, in addition to showing off the land, I'll show you how the ranch works. If you're interested, that is."

"I'm totally interested. I want to see everything."

Isaac grinned. "Then it's a date."

Chapter Five

Isaac watched for Savannah's reaction to his referring to their next meeting as a date. He knew that she was cautious, and given the horrific way that she'd lost her husband and child, he understood her reluctance to grow close to anyone. In her situation, he might react the same way. Before Lisa's death, he had never lost anyone close to him. He was only now learning how insidious grief was. He could be happily working one minute and the next he would feel a punch to the gut as overwhelming sorrow struck him. And he was occasionally struck with the irrational fear that he would be killed, leaving Mia alone again.

"I wouldn't exactly call it a date," she said softly.

"No? Why not?"

"Because right now it's just words. We haven't set a time or place."

"So you're saying it's too nebulous?"

She glanced at him over her shoulder, her eyebrows raised. Then she gave a mischievous smile that lit up her face. "Yes. So how about we set a date and time, cowboy?"

He smiled slowly. This was the playful woman lurking inside the mourning widow. The woman she would have been had tragedy not intervened. "I think that is the perfect solution to this problem."

"So when do you suggest?" Her voice was flirtatious. Practically a purr, and he responded in kind.

"I'm free whenever you are. I would suggest now, but I have a feeling my brother wouldn't approve of me leaving my work half-done."

"You don't strike me as the type to do that."

"Trust me, I'm not. I give my all to everything." He realized he had slipped from the father mode he'd fought so hard to develop into his old habit of flirting. Since Savannah had started it, he didn't see the problem with enjoying themselves.

"I'll make a note of that."

He nodded. "Make sure you do."

The air fairly crackled with sexual tension and Isaac warned himself to tread carefully. Savannah might be playing with him now, but he imagined she would be battling her emotions later. She'd backed away whenever he got too close to her.

He glanced over at Scout, who was walking happily beside them. They were near Savannah's cabin, and he was sorry that their time together was coming to a close. He enjoyed having Savannah in his arms. She was so soft, and her round bottom was pressed against him, leaving him battling his arousal. It was a struggle to hide the hot desire that was surging through him, but if she noticed, she didn't mention it.

He inhaled a whiff of Savannah's sweet scent. She smelled like roses. Her fragrance was tantalizing and filled Isaac with longing. He'd desired women before, but nothing came close to this intensity. But then, Savannah was so different from every other woman. She reached his heart in a way that he hadn't known was possible.

He'd never been in love before, so he didn't know exactly what it felt like. But he'd seen Miles fall in love with Jillian, so he knew what being in love looked like. The vulnerability that came with the complete surrender of your heart. The willingness to open yourself up to someone and trust that they'll take care to not hurt you.

Not that he thought he was in love with Savannah. He knew that love grew over time. It didn't just hit you over the head when you least expected it. If anything, he was in the throes of a major crush. Given the situation, he would enjoy the sensation until the emotions burned themselves out.

He guided Samson to the cabin's stairs. "Wait until I dismount, then I'll help you."

"Okay." She sighed audibly. "I'm sort of sorry that the ride is over."

"I would take you on a longer ride, but this is probably a good length for the first time out. See how you feel in the morning. Better safe than sorry."

"You sound like an old grandma. Or like you think I am."

"Believe me, I would never mistake you for an old lady."

She seemed mollified by his answer, so he dismounted Samson.

"You did that so easily," she said. "I have a feeling it's harder than it looks."

He shrugged. "I've been riding since I could walk, so it's like second nature to me. But I'm going to help you. Before you know it, you'll be on the ground. Just sling your right leg over Samson's back and twist a bit."

She gave him an odd look. "Uh-oh."

"What do you mean *uh-oh*?"

"I can't move my leg."

He grinned. "I guess you're going to have to live on Samson's back for the rest of your life."

She narrowed her eyes in an attempt to look fierce. Instead, she looked cute. "Don't make me hurt you."

"Just kidding." He walked around his horse and

lifted Savannah's knee. She wiggled in the saddle and then swung around. He circled Samson to stand on the horse's left side. Instead of instructing her, he grabbed her by the waist. She placed her hands on his shoulders and he lowered her to the ground.

Once he knew she was steady on her feet, he could have released her, yet something inside him wouldn't let him. Apparently, she felt the same because her hands remained on his shoulders. He was tempted to kiss her, but feared that would send her racing away. Despite the fact that holding her felt like heaven, he let his hands drop to his sides. Her eyes widened as if she'd only just realized how close they were to each other, and she slid her hands from his shoulders.

"Thanks for the ride home. I appreciate it."

"It was my pleasure."

"I should probably give Scout some water."

"He can wait a minute while we firm up details."

"Of?"

He doubted that she'd forgotten, but he decided to play along. "Our date. Horseback riding so you can see the ranch. And then our other date to show you ranch operations."

"So, two dates?"

"Yes." Technically he could show her everything at the same time, but he wasn't going to volunteer that information. "What days work for you?"

An odd expression crossed her face and then vanished. It occurred to him that he didn't know what she did for a living. Did she work remotely? Or at all? He hoped she at least had a hobby, but he wasn't going to pry. He hated to think that she spent countless days and nights alone with only her grief for companionship.

"I'm free every day. What about you?"

"Like I said, I'm ready when you are. Tomorrow's Sunday and I'm off all day. If it's okay with you, I'll pick you up in the morning around ten." Isaac knew she was skittish and didn't want to give her too much time for fear she'd talk herself out of it.

Isaac hadn't gone on a date since Mia had come to live with him. He knew his mother had never approved of his previous lifestyle, although she had never said a negative word to him. But she had told him more than once that he was doing a great job as Mia's father. She'd also told him that it was okay for him to go out on occasion, too, promising that she would watch Mia. This would be a good time to take her up on it.

"With two horses? Can you do that?"

"Easily. Or I can drive here, pick you up and bring you back to the stable so you can choose your own horse."

"I like that idea."

He tipped his hat. "Then I'll see you in the morning."

"It's a date."

He waited until she was inside her cabin before heading home. It wasn't his usual type of first date, but he believed it would be the most fun he'd had in a long time.

Savannah stood in the front room, peering out the window while she watched Isaac ride away. She couldn't believe she'd been sitting with his arms wrapped around her waist, but she had. And she'd savored every second of it. She waited for regret or panic to rear their ugly head, but they didn't. The only thing she felt was anticipation.

Scout barked, stirring Savannah out of her stupor. She filled his bowl with fresh water and gave him a treat. The walk had zapped his energy, and he settled on his bed, content to gnaw on a rubber bone. Unlike Scout, Savannah was suddenly bursting with energy. The cabin was spotless, so cleaning it was out of the question—not to mention unappealing.

She paced to the window and back. Finally, she decided to bake. Although she was a serviceable cook at best, she was a tremendous baker. She hadn't baked once since she'd moved here, but there was a time when she'd baked regularly. She'd made scrumptious cakes each Sunday that the three of them had eaten for dessert the following days. Tony had loved her chocolate chip cookies. She could practically hear the echo of his laughter as he took his first delicious bite; could see his face, covered with chocolate and crumbs. He always ate them way too fast, and one was never enough. *One more, Mommy. Please, one more.* More often than not, she'd given in to his pleas.

Savannah grabbed a cookie sheet from under the counter and began gathering the ingredients. She debated between cookies and two kinds of cakes before deciding on cookies.

She turned on the radio as she worked, humming along with the music. When the song that Isaac had been singing to Mia in the store came over the air, her heart stuttered. Isaac had a nice voice and she'd been impressed by his ability to stay on key. Listening to the words of the love song, she couldn't help but smile. The lyrics might not be remotely appropriate for a lullaby, but they had a definite appeal to the woman in her. She imagined Isaac serenading her with the song, and her knees wobbled.

"Stop being so foolish," she whispered. Isaac wasn't going to woo her with love songs. Nor did she want him to. That would be crossing the line from friendship into something more. She'd already erased one line when she'd become his friend after saying she wouldn't. But she was drawing a new line here. If she became romantically involved with him, her heart wouldn't survive if something went wrong. And in life, something always went wrong. The best way to avoid being devastated was to keep the walls up around her heart.

That was good in theory, but it was becoming harder in practice. Isaac was attractive in ways she hadn't anticipated. She'd expected charm, but not the depth of his understanding. His compassion. He was a better man than she could have ever hoped. And darn, wasn't that as big a turn-on as his gorgeous face and sexy body?

Although Darren hadn't been her first lover, he'd been her last. They'd planned on growing old together, so she hadn't thought of ever having another. Never in her wildest dreams had she imagined that she could feel desire for anyone other than her husband. But then, she'd never imagined that Darren would be snatched away from her so cruelly. He might not be here with her physically, but that didn't mean her love had died. It simply no longer had anyone to receive it.

But there could be.

The idea came from out of nowhere—and she quickly banished it. She knew there were many men in the world, and that the possibility of meeting one she could love was great. But love didn't come with assurances. And she needed assurances.

Enough of that, she thought, and forced her attention back to the task at hand. Mixing flour, eggs and sugar was second nature and the buttery scents and the familiar activity brought good feelings. Before long, she had whipped up two dozen chocolate chip cookies and slid them into the oven. The sweet aroma filled the air while she mixed the ingredients for the peanut butter cookies. By the time she pulled the cookie sheet out of the oven, she was ready to slide in the next one.

Her mouth watered as she waited for the cookies to cool on the wire rack. She poured a cup of milk, grabbed a cookie, and then bit into it. She closed her eyes as she savored the gooey goodness. She missed this simple joy.

When she pulled out the last batch of cookies, she was suffused with a contentment that she hadn't experienced in ages. The world didn't seem as bleak as it had yesterday. Although part of the reason was the pleasure she'd derived from baking desserts, she knew Isaac played a big part as well. He'd brought sunshine back into her life.

"Where did you vanish to? I thought you were going to help me with that calf."

Isaac had been cleaning Samson's saddle. Now he paused and looked over at Miles. His brother didn't look particularly perturbed. Just curious. "Do you remember Savannah?"

Miles nodded. "The beautiful neighbor with the dog. The one who shot you down." He grinned.

"She went out for a walk and got lost. She ended up on the ranch again. I ran across her and gave her a ride back home."

"Really?"

Isaac didn't like the tone of his brother's voice. "Yes. You have a problem with it?"

"No. And why are you reacting like that?"

"Like what?"

"Offended. As if I insulted you. Or her." Miles smiled slowly. "That's it, right? You think I'm casting aspersions on her character."

That was exactly it. Wasn't it just like Miles to notice? But Miles always did have a way of reading him. Perhaps it came from being the quiet type who observed more than he participated. Or maybe it came from being the big brother. Whatever, it was annoying. "She's a nice woman."

"They always are."

"What does that mean?"

"Women like you. And you definitely like them."

"I haven't been out since Mia came to live with me. So what are you accusing me of?"

Miles held his hands in front of him. "I'm not accusing you of anything. I think it's noble that you've put your life on hold to take care of Mia. You're a great father. Nobody can question that. But you're still…"

"I'm still what?"

"You. You're still you."

"And I like the company of women."

Miles nodded.

"You know, I would expect this from Nathan-the-Perfect. But not you. I thought you would see me as more than a player. I guess I expected too much of you."

Isaac resumed cleaning Samson's saddle, scrubbing harder than was necessary. He couldn't believe how badly his brother's words hurt him. Everyone knew that Miles was a devoted father. Isaac had done his best to live up to the standard Miles had set. He might still be struggling, but he thought he'd been doing a good job overall. Too bad his brother didn't see that.

He felt a hand on his shoulder. He shook it off and kept working.

"I'm not leaving, so you may as well stop rubbing a hole in the leather and turn around and look at me."

When it came to being stubborn, Miles and Isaac were equally matched. Isaac had no doubt his brother would stand there all night if necessary, which meant that Isaac would have to stand there all night too, so he spun around. "What?"

"I didn't mean to offend you. If it sounded as if I was saying you are anything less than a great father, I apologize. I'm not criticizing you as a father. Or as a man, for that matter. There's nothing wrong with you spending time with Savannah. I think it's a good idea. Children need two parents if they can have them."

"Wait a minute. I'm not talking about marrying her. We barely know each other."

"Okay." Miles nodded, letting the subject drop as if wary of starting another disagreement. "Are we good?"

"Yeah. Sorry for being so sensitive."

"Lack of sleep will do that."

"Tell me about it. Suddenly, Mia is all about the nightlife."

"You're raising a party animal."

"Not my sweet girl. She's going to be a good student who hangs out at the library and goes to bed at a respectable hour."

"One can only hope." Miles turned to go, took two steps and swiveled around. "What are you doing tomorrow? Jillian and I are taking the kids to the movie in town followed by the obligatory face painting. You should bring Mia. She might enjoy it."

Isaac shook his head. "I can't. I have plans."

"Plans?" That word held so many undercurrents, but Isaac knew Miles wouldn't ask for details.

Isaac chuckled. "I'm taking Savannah horseback riding. I'm going to show her around the ranch."

"That sounds like fun."

Suddenly, Isaac found himself wanting to talk about Savannah. "I really like her. She's different from other women."

"Meaning she's not falling all over herself to be with you."

"That's one way of putting it. She's literally run away from me." Although it was not remotely funny,

Isaac laughed at the perplexed look on his brother's face and explained his encounters with Savannah. He also shared a bit about her background.

"Wow. She's suffered a lot of heartache. Are you sure you want to get involved with her?"

"Truthfully? No. I'm scared of doing or saying the wrong thing and hurting her even more. But something tells me it's all going to be worth it."

"Then I wish you the best of luck."

"That's it? You're not going to try to dissuade me?"

"Nah. That's Nathan's job. One Mr. Negative in the family is enough, don't you think?"

"More than enough." Isaac was still trying to get over his bitterness toward his oldest brother. It stung knowing that Nathan didn't believe Isaac had what it took to be a good father. He had hoped that after seeing him in action, Nathan would admit to being wrong, but he hadn't said a word. Perhaps he still believed what he'd said.

Isaac put the saddle away and then walked with Miles to their parents' house. As they went, he put away all thoughts of Nathan and turned his mind to something positive.

His upcoming date with Savannah.

Chapter Six

Savannah sat on her front porch, eagerly awaiting Isaac's appearance. A plastic wrapped plate of chocolate chip and peanut butter cookies sat on the table beside her. It had been chilly earlier this morning, and the air had been crisp. Now the sun was shining brightly, warming the air. Her long-sleeved T-shirt and jeans were all she needed.

She'd told herself not to make a big deal out of the outing, but she hadn't been completely successful. There was no mistaking her anticipation. She'd awakened early this morning with butterflies in her stomach that had yet to calm down.

Her reaction didn't make sense. It wasn't as if this was a date in the traditional sense of the word. They were simply two people going horseback riding on his ranch. That was surprising enough. Savannah had never been the outdoorsy type. She'd preferred dinners at fancy restaurants and spa days. And if sports were involved, she preferred to spectate, not participate. This was a definitely out of character for her.

But then, everything in her life was different now. She'd gone from living in a college town to living on an isolated ranch. From having a full social life to spending all of her time alone. Darren and Tony's deaths had turned her into a different person. Her interests had died with them. She couldn't claim to have new interests because she hadn't been a bit interested in anything until Isaac had come into her life.

She heard his SUV a few seconds before she saw it, and ran a hand over her hair. When she realized what she was doing, she stopped. She didn't need to worry about her appearance.

Grabbing the plate of treats, she stood and waited for Isaac as he approached. He smiled and her heart skipped a beat in response. Dressed in faded jeans that showcased his muscular thighs, a plaid shirt that fit his massive chest and shoulders perfectly, and his ever-present cowboy hat, he could have been any rancher in town. But her reaction to him emphasized that he wasn't just any random cowboy. He was Isaac Montgomery, a kind and charming man. A man she was attracted to.

"Hi," he said, when he was close enough for her to hear. He put a booted foot on the lower of the three stairs and glanced at her. His nearness stalled her breath. "Ready to go?"

"Yes. Oh, and I'd like to drop off some cookies at your parents' house. You know, to thank them for letting me visit their ranch." She recalled how his mother had dropped off a cake, and was happy to be in a position to reciprocate.

"They'll appreciate them. Of course, since I'm the one doing the showing, I should at least get a cookie."

She put a finger on her chin and pretended to think about it. "I suppose that would be okay. After your parents get theirs."

"Fair enough." He took the plate in one hand and held his other out to her. His hand was warm and calloused. She'd seen him work hard, so she wasn't surprised by the texture. She was surprised, however, by the spark of electricity that shot from her fingers, up her arm and into her stomach at the casual contact.

Intense guilt battered her. She shouldn't be responding like this to him. She pulled her hand away. If Isaac noticed her reaction, he let it pass without comment. He simply opened the truck door and stepped aside so she could climb inside.

Lecturing herself not to overreact every time they brushed each other, Savannah fastened her seat belt. Today wouldn't be any fun if she was all tied up in knots.

"I'm going to put the dessert on the floor behind your seat."

"Okay."

Once they were underway, Isaac glanced over at her. As usual, he appeared perfectly relaxed. His calm demeanor put her at ease.

"Since you're a novice rider, I have three horses for you to choose from. They're all gentle, and you'll be perfectly safe with any of them."

"Do you have any horses that aren't gentle?"

"Yes. We have some horses that are really spirited. There are a few that absolutely love running. And others that will buck you off if given the chance. We also have a couple of new horses that are skittish and who have to learn to trust again."

"Really?" She turned in her seat to get a better look at him.

"Horses are a lot like people. They have their own personalities. Their own lived experiences. When a horse has been traumatized or mistreated, it is important to give that horse special care. You can't ignore its history and treat it as you would a horse that has lived a perfect life."

"Is that the philosophy of Isaac Montgomery?"

"That's the Edward Montgomery philosophy that he passed on to me, my brothers and everyone who works on our ranch."

"It's a nice philosophy." One she agreed with.

"We're here."

He turned onto a long driveway, driving past a magnificent home with gorgeous landscaping, not stopping until he was at the back of the house. The gorgeous yard resembled a resort. There was a massive swimming pool with a waterfall at one end, a large brick patio with lawn chairs and couches arranged in inviting seating areas, two cabanas, and a massive hot tub. An outdoor kitchen completed the setup.

"Wow."

He smiled. "My parents love to entertain. Friends and neighbors are always welcome. If you ever get lonely in your cabin, feel free to drop by."

She nodded, although she wasn't ready to take that kind of step. Just letting Isaac into her life required a huge leap of faith. She wasn't ready to add more people to the mix. Sure, she got lonely, even more so now that the numbness had begun to wear off, but it was a loneliness for her family. The company of random people wouldn't fill that hole.

An older couple whom she presumed were Isaac's parents was sitting at the table.

"Come meet my parents," he said, confirming her guess. "My father has a sweet tooth that is second to none, so when he sees your desserts, he'll be your biggest fan."

She wondered what Isaac had told them about her

and then decided she was worrying over nothing. It wasn't as if he were bringing her home to *meet his parents*. He was simply being polite.

As they got nearer, she spied a playpen that she hadn't noticed before. Mia was inside, pounding on a musical toy and chanting along as if singing. Seeing the baby made her heart seize. Then Mia gave a sweet smile and began to bounce on her bottom, and Savannah blew out a breath.

"Dadadada."

"Hey, sweetie." Isaac picked up Mia and kissed her cheek. Knowing that Isaac wasn't the baby's biological father made his obvious love for her that much more touching. Mia would grow up knowing that she was treasured. No child could ask for more.

Holding his daughter in one arm, he gestured to Savannah. Mia had knocked his hat on the ground and had a fistful of his locks. He picked up his hat, set it on the table and then pulled his hair from Mia's hand. "Mom, Dad, this is Savannah Rogers. She's renting the Duncan cabin. Savannah, these are my parents, Michelle and Edward Montgomery."

"We met once before," Michelle said, smiling.

"I remember. Thank you for the cake. I brought a couple dozen cookies—peanut butter and chocolate chip." She set the treats on the table.

"Ook?" Mia said, twisting to look at Savannah. Her eyes lit up and her grin broadened. Mia was as charming as her father.

"Not for you," Isaac said. "You'll be bouncing off the walls."

"One taste won't hurt anything," Michelle said.

Isaac rolled his eyes and Savannah couldn't help but laugh at his exasperated expression. Apparently, he was still learning that grandmothers always won.

"It's very nice to meet you," Edward said. He grabbed one of each kind of cookie. "These will go perfect with my coffee. Thank you."

"You're welcome."

"Isaac says you're going out riding today."

"Yes. I've never been horseback riding before and I'm looking forward to it."

"I'm sure you'll enjoy yourself. And feel free to drop by anytime you want to ride."

"That's a very generous offer. I should make sure I like it, first."

"That's a given. We have the best horses in Colorado. And the most scenic land too."

"On that note, we're going to leave. Don't worry, Dad, I'm going to show Savannah all of the best spots. Thanks again for watching Mia for me."

"Hold on one second," Michelle said. "I need to get something from the kitchen."

Savannah glanced at Isaac, who shrugged. He kissed Mia's cheek once more and then set her back into the playpen. She picked up a blue plastic maraca and began to shake it. The sound delighted her and she laughed and shook it again.

"I packed you a lunch," Michelle said, walking over to them. She had a large wicker basket in her hands. "Be sure to take a blanket with you."

"I'm way ahead of you. I already have one."

Michelle patted his cheek. "Of course you do."

"We'll see you later," Isaac said.

Savannah waved and strode beside Isaac across the patio to a paved walk that veered off in three directions. They took the middle path that led straight ahead.

"If you go to the left, you'll end up at the barns. The path to the right leads to the river, although it ends way before then."

When they reached the stables, he led her past the building to a fenced-in area that went as far as the eye could see. "The horses are free to roam in and out whenever they want in the daytime. Buttercup, Wildfire and Shadow are the three horses I selected for you."

He pointed to the horses as he spoke. Each was more beautiful than the next. "I can't choose. Which one do you think I'll like the best?"

He looked at her, slowly perusing her from head to toe. Although her skin began to burn as if his eyes held fire, she stood still. She had no idea what he was looking for, if anything, but when her eyes met his, they sparkled with mischief. "I think you'll like Wildfire best."

"Then that's the one I want."

Although the gate wasn't far away, he hopped the fence and crossed to the horses. He reached up and rubbed the brown one on the mane and then led the horse through the gate and over to Savannah. Even though she had ridden a horse with Isaac, she was a bit apprehensive about riding on her own.

"Don't be nervous," Isaac said, as if reading her mind. "You're going to be perfectly safe. Okay?"

She nodded.

Isaac whistled and then she heard thundering hooves as Samson raced across the corral. When he reached the gate, Isaac opened it and let his horse out.

"You trained your horse to come when you whistle?"

"Yep. Now let's get them saddled so we can head out. There's so much to see and so little time to see it." He put a blanket and then a saddle on each of the horses and then helped her onto Wildfire's back. He adjusted the stirrups and handed her the reins. He then hopped onto Samson's back. "Before we leave, we're going to walk around the corral so you can get comfortable, okay?"

She nodded. "That sounds like a plan."

"Don't worry. Samson is a good leader. Wildfire is going to follow his lead."

Isaac and Samson began walking with Wildfire behind them. After ten minutes of ambling so slowly they might not even be moving, Savannah wanted to pick up the pace. "Can we go faster?"

"Feeling the need for speed?" Isaac asked, glancing over his shoulder.

"Maybe not speed, but a turtle just passed us. And it was mocking us."

"We can't have that," Isaac said and then led her through the corral gate. He jumped down, closed it, and was back on his horse with impressive speed. He shook his reins and gently kicked Samson's side. The horse walked more quickly. She shook her reins and tapped Wildfire's side, making him speed up. Isaac steered his horse so that they were now riding side by side. They were going faster now, but not fast enough for Savannah to worry about falling off.

The ride was exhilarating, and she found herself laughing out loud. "This is so much fun."

"I'm glad you're enjoying yourself," Isaac said. She heard the sincerity in his voice and her heart warmed.

"I am."

"Do you think you can last for another twenty or thirty minutes? I want to show you one of my favorite places, but you can only get there on horseback."

She nodded, excitement surging through her.

As they rode across the ranch, Isaac pointed out features as if he were a tour guide leading her in a foreign country. That was close to accurate. She was a city girl, so this was pretty foreign to her. A

Get up to 4
FREE FABULOUS BOOKS
You Love!

To thank you for being a loyal reader we'd like to send you up to 4 FREE BOOKS, absolutely free when you try the Harlequin Reader Service.

Just write "YES" on the Loyal Reader Voucher and we'll send you 2 free books from each series you choose and Free Mystery Gifts, altogether worth over $20.

Try **Harlequin® Special Edition** and get 2 books featuring comfort and strength in the support of loved ones and enjoying the journey no matter what life throws your way.

Try **Harlequin® Heartwarming™ Larger-Print** and get 2 books featuring uplifting stories where the bonds of friendship, family and community unite.

Or **TRY BOTH and get 2 books from each series!**

Your free books are completely free, even the shipping! If you continue with your subscription, you can look forward to curated monthly shipments of brand-new books from your selected series, always at a discount off the cover price! Plus you can cancel any time.

So don't miss out, return your Loyal Readers Voucher today to get your Free books.

Pam Powers

LOYAL READER
FREE BOOKS VOUCHER

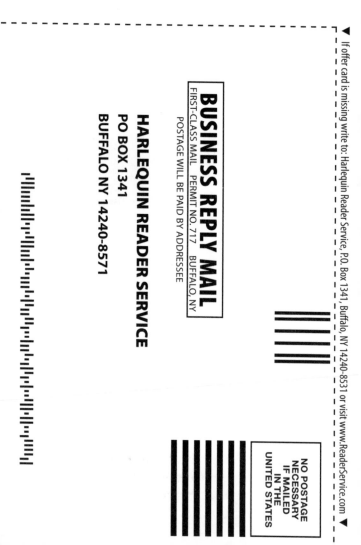

year might have passed since she'd come to Colorado, but she'd lived most of that in seclusion, just leaving the cabin when necessary and very rarely stepping into the yard. Only now was she beginning to pay attention to her beautiful surroundings.

The ranch really was breathtaking and as impressive as Isaac had promised. No wonder he and his father were so proud of it.

It would be easy to berate herself for ignoring the beauty in her own backyard for so long, but she wouldn't. She'd been caught in the fog of grief and getting out of bed had been all she could manage most days. Now, though, the fog was clearing, and she was finding small pleasure in life again. Life wasn't as good as it had once been, and she didn't believe it ever would be without Darren and Tony there to share it with her. But it wasn't as miserable as it had been.

Twenty minutes later, Isaac slowed his horse, and she did the same. "It's just over the hill."

He was grinning broadly, and Savannah could feel his excitement. It was contagious and she found herself smiling back at him. There was a lightness in her spirit that hadn't been there previously, and she intended to experience it to the fullest before it faded away.

As they climbed the hill, her anticipation grew. When they reached the top, they stopped, and Savannah looked around. It was absolutely spectacular. The view in front of her was like something out of a dream. The green grass was interspersed with colorful wildflowers that danced in the breeze. Mature, leafy trees lined the meadow like soldiers guarding the peace. A family of deer drank from a stream while rabbits and squirrels chased each other across the grass. A breeze blew, perfuming the air with the delightful scent of the flowers.

"What do you think?" Isaac asked as he dismounted.

"There are no words. No wonder you like it. If I lived on the ranch, I think I would spend every free moment here."

"I come as often as I can. Especially when I need to think. It's easy to clear my mind here. And when life gets rough, I come here to decompress."

"You're very lucky to have a space like this."

"You have an open invitation to come here any time you want."

She laughed as he helped her down. "Did you forget that I'm the one who got lost in my own backyard? There's no way I can find my way here on my own."

"Then call me and I'll bring you here."

"Is that right? You'll just drop whatever you're doing and bring me here?"

"Yes."

His eyes bore into hers and the blood began to race through her veins. She didn't quite know what to say. He must have sensed that she was overwhelmed because he changed the subject. "I don't know about you, but I worked up an appetite. What do you say we stop here and eat lunch?"

They had only been riding for about ninety minutes, but she was hungry. Her stomach had danced with anticipation this morning and she hadn't been able to do more than swallow four or five bites of dry toast and chase them down with a few sips of grapefruit juice. "Sounds good. What do we have?"

"I have no idea. My mother is a great cook, so no matter what it is, you can count on it being delicious."

Isaac spread a blanket on the grass and then took the basket from Samson's back. He opened the basket and began pulling out plastic containers. He stacked them then took out two plates, silverware and several bottles of flavored water. Once everything was in the center of the blanket, he and Savannah settled and began to open containers. With each one, she became more delighted. There were chicken salad sandwiches, cold fried chicken, strawberries, grapes, pasta salad, cheese and chocolate.

"Wow. Your mom packed a lot. She knows it's just the two of us, right?"

"Yes. But working on a ranch often involves hard, physical labor that builds an appetite. Over the years, my mother got used to cooking big meals. My brothers and I have our own houses on the ranch, but Mom always prepares a lot, just in case one of us drops in for dinner."

"That's sweet."

Isaac shrugged. "That's Mom."

"What was it like growing up on a ranch?"

"Fun. From the outside, it might look like we're isolated out here and, in a way, we are. The land as far as you can see belongs to our family, so we don't have a lot of close neighbors. But kids lived on the other ranches and we often got together and played. We fished, swam, sailed and played ball in the summer. In the winter, we skied, snowboarded, ice-skated. Whatever winter activity you can think of, we did.

"Aspen Creek is a major resort town now, but it wasn't always. When we were growing up, it had more of a small-town feel with very few tourists. Kids got together for dances at the park fieldhouse. Sometimes we went to Denver for sporting events or to see movies that didn't come here."

"It sounds idyllic."

"For the most part, it was. But people are the same all over, so we had conflicts from time to time. Nothing major, though." He bit and chewed a piece of chicken before he continued. "Are you thinking of making Aspen Creek your permanent residence?"

She shrugged. That was the good thing about Isaac knowing about her past. She didn't have to give him vague, meaningless answers that didn't say anything. Somehow, Isaac had become a trusted friend, so she could be honest. "I'm not sure. When I came here, I wasn't looking to put down roots. I was looking for respite from the pain." She picked a grape from the container and stared at it for a moment. "I wanted to die. But since that wasn't possible, I left Madison. I couldn't live there without Darren and Tony. Finding a new hometown and making new friends wasn't something that I had even considered."

"And now?"

She took a sip of strawberry-flavored water before responding. "I still don't know. You're the first friend that I've made since I moved here. To be honest, I didn't want to connect with anyone. Despite my best efforts to keep you out of my life, we have become friends."

He grinned and dimples flashed in his cheeks. "So, you're saying I'm charming as a lamb and I won you over."

She poked his hard shoulder. "You're more like a battering ram breaking through my defenses."

He threw back his head and laughed. "Whatever works."

"Clearly, there's no offending you."

"Was that what you were trying to do? I actually thought you were complimenting me."

"I was. Before I realized how huge your ego was."

"Not hardly. I'm the baby of the family. When I

was younger, I couldn't keep up with my brothers, so I had to develop other skills. Charm seemed to work best."

"And now?"

"I'm just as big as they are. Of course, now I'm not trying to keep up with them."

"What are you trying to do?"

His lips turned down attractively as he pondered that question. When he spoke, his voice didn't contain the humor it had before. It was lower. Serious. "I'm trying to be the best father that Mia can have. I hope that I can somehow love her enough to make up for the mother she lost before she even had a chance to know her."

Wow. And there it was. She had been doing her best to keep things light and he'd dropped an emotional bomb on her. "How do you think you're doing?"

"Some days are better than others. It's hard to know because she can't talk. She can't tell me how she's feeling or what she needs from me."

"From what I've seen, she's happy. I saw the way her eyes lit up when she saw you. She loves you and she feels loved by you."

"Thanks." He swallowed hard, clearly moved by her words. Then he covered her hand with his. "How does seeing Mia affect you? It must be hard being around children after you've lost your own son."

"A few days ago I would have told you that it was

like a knife in my heart," she said before she could stop the words. But then, there was no reason to lie.

"And now?"

"There's still a pang."

He sucked in a breath and gave her hand a gentle squeeze. "I'm sorry."

"Don't be. You weren't the one driving the truck that hit my family."

"What happened? Or is it too painful to talk about? I don't want to ruin this day for you."

"You're not ruining anything. And it's not as if not talking about it makes me forget."

He nodded, but didn't say anything.

She knew if she changed the subject to anything else, he would go with it without comment. Knowing that only made her like him more. Trust him more. Make her need to resist him more.

"It was a Saturday afternoon. Darren and Tony had what they called man-time while I went to the spa or shopping. They would go out to a local restaurant for breakfast and go to the park to play if the weather was nice. I would meet up with them later. We'd play for a while and then go to lunch. Then we'd go to the movies or the museum or do some other fun activity."

"That sounds wonderful."

"It was."

"How old was your son?"

"Three and a half. He was so happy and energetic. Just the best little boy you could ever imagine." A tear must have slipped from her eye because she felt a napkin brush against her cheek. She sniffed and looked up at Isaac. His gaze was filled with sympathy—and understanding. He didn't press her to continue, but rather waited in silence while she gathered herself.

"Anyway, that day was beautiful. My girlfriends and I met up at the spa. We had a great time. I remember laughing with them while we got pedicures. We were standing at the front desk, paying our bills, when my phone rang." She closed her eyes against the remembered pain of that moment. "It was the father of one of Tony's friends from preschool. He and Darren had arranged for the kids to play that morning. Tony and Darren were in the intersection when a drunk driver ran a red light and crashed into them. One of my friends drove me to the park. We pulled up at the same time as the paramedics were pronouncing them dead. There was nothing they could do."

She heard Isaac's intake of breath. "Oh no."

"And just like that, they were gone. I'd just seen them at breakfast. Tony was excited about playing with his friend, Christopher. That's all he'd talked about. Playing football with Christopher. Darren and I shared a smile. Then I kissed them both goodbye. I didn't know it would be forever."

"I don't know the words to tell you how very sorry I am."

"There are no words. Besides, words can't bring my family back."

"How long ago was this?"

"Four hundred and forty-seven days."

His eyebrows rose and his mouth dropped open. And then he snapped it shut. She knew he was holding back. That he wanted to comment on the fact that she knew exactly how many days it had been. Why wouldn't she know the moment joy was snatched from her? The day that love died?

"It seemed as if the entire town mourned with me. Darren had been well-liked. He was the kind of man you called when you needed help. The church could barely hold all the people who'd wanted to attend the funeral. I appreciated their support at the same time I wanted everyone to leave me alone to grieve. I didn't want to shake another hand and hear a remembered kindness Darren had done for someone. Or what a sweet child Tony had been. How much they'd be missed. How was I supposed to find the right thing to say to anyone? I know they were sorry. I know they meant what they were saying. But…" She shook her head in despair. "All I knew was that my life was over. And there was nothing anyone could say to make it better. Or change it."

She glanced at him. "I suppose you think I'm a horrible, selfish person."

"I think you suffered a loss no one should ever have to endure. I haven't lost anyone that close to me, and I certainly haven't lost two people at once. Who am I to judge you?"

"After the funeral, people went back to their lives. I knew they would, but I didn't expect to feel the resentment I did. Not that I wanted anyone else to be as miserable as I was or to suffer the kind of loss that I had. I wouldn't wish that on my worst enemy. But it felt as if they had forgotten Darren and Tony.

"Before long, people began to have expectations of me. They wanted me to go back to work. To keep busy. As if being busy would keep me from realizing that my son and husband had been killed. As if teaching a course on Shakespeare would suddenly wipe all the pain from my life."

She paused. He didn't fill the space with platitudes. Instead, he simply sat there and waited. Held her hand.

"I tried to go back to work, but I couldn't teach. I couldn't focus. Couldn't make myself care whether or not my students learned that *Romeo and Juliet* was a tragedy and not a romance. So I took a leave of absence. But my friends and family had been right about one thing. Sitting in the house was not good for me. No matter where I looked, I saw Darren and Tony. Heard their laughter. Saw Darren standing at the grill, making the ribs that he was so proud of.

"And Tony. Reminders of him were everywhere.

In the living room where he took his first step. The pencil lines on the wall where we marked his growth every month. Some might have found the memories comforting, but they only reminded me of what I had lost. What I would never have again. So I put my house up for sale, then got in my car and began to drive. I didn't know where I was going, I just wanted to get away. Away from the memories, I guess. When I arrived in Aspen Creek, things fell together and I rented the cabin. You know the rest."

Isaac shook his head. "I'm so sorry for all that you've lost, Savannah. No one should have to go through what you did."

"Thank you."

"That brings me back to my question. Do you think you might stay in Aspen Creek?"

Isaac held his breath as he waited for Savannah's response. He didn't know why it was so important to him that she stay in town, but it was. Despite her attempt to keep him at a distance, the more time he spent with Savannah, the closer he felt to her. It would be easy to fall in love with her. Given all that she'd suffered, he doubted that she would be able to love him in return. He was many things, but a glutton for punishment wasn't one of them. More than that, he had Mia to consider. He couldn't bring a woman into her life who wouldn't be able to love her as much as she deserved to be loved. Savannah had been clear that she wasn't sure she could welcome another child into her life. So he should be the one who kept his distance from her.

Even so, he couldn't make himself breathe without hearing her answer.

"I'm not sure. I know that at some point, I need to pick up the pieces of my life, but I can't make myself go back to Madison. Not yet."

"Why do you have to go back to Wisconsin? Can you pick up your life here?"

"What would I do here?"

"The same thing you did there."

"I'm an English Literature professor."

"We have universities here. Not in Aspen Creek, but in Colorado. You could teach in one of them."

"I can't do that."

"Why not?"

She shrugged, unable to come up with an answer.

"Because you came here to get away from life?" he suggested gently.

"Yes."

"But there's nothing that says you can't make a new life here. You get to choose what that life will look like, of course. You don't have to teach again if you don't want to. You don't have to do anything you don't want."

"I don't know."

"That's fair. And you don't have to make major life decisions today. In fact, let's declare the rest of today to be exclusively fun. No more deep conversations. Let's just ride and enjoy ourselves."

"That's a plan that I can get behind."

He lay on his back, one arm behind his head, and stared at the sky. Several puffy clouds floated lazily across the boundless blue. He pointed to one. "What does that look like to you?"

She lay beside him, her shoulder brushing against his. His body stirred in response, but he forced himself to concentrate on the clouds and not the desirable woman lying beside him, her soft scent tempting him.

She looked up and then grinned. "A cloud?" He poked her side and she giggled. "Well, you did ask."

"Okay, smarty-pants. What does the cloud look like?"

She wrinkled her brow as she studied. "I suppose it looks like a train."

"That's what I thought." He looked at another one. "Does that look like a duck to you?"

"No. That's more of a chicken."

"Are you kidding?" He leaned up on one elbow and stared at her. It would be so easy to kiss her. "You are definitely a city girl if you don't know a duck when you see one."

"It doesn't have a beak. How can it be a duck without a beak?"

Chickens had beaks, something this city girl obviously didn't know and that he wasn't going to point out. He looked back at the cloud. The large beak, which had been there before, had melted away and now the cloud did look more like a chicken. Not that he was going to admit to it when she was gloating like the queen of the cloud game.

She poked him in the side. "Nothing to say there?"

Her eyes sparkled with mirth. The wind blew her hair into her face, and he automatically brushed it behind her ear. The instant his hand touched her skin, an electric charge shot through his body. All reason fled and he reacted purely on instinct. Caressing her cheek, he looked down at her. Her eyes had drifted shut. Though there were a thousand reasons why he shouldn't, he leaned down and kissed her soft lips. He had intended the kiss to be gentle. Brief. But the moment his mouth touched hers, heat blazed to life. Even so, he would have backed away if she hadn't opened her mouth to him. Immediately, his tongue swept inside, tangling with hers.

She tasted of strawberries with a hint of chocolate and her own personal sweetness. He deepened the kiss, pulling her against him. This was what he'd wanted to do from the moment he'd laid eyes on her. Back then, he hadn't known anything about her. Not even her name. He recalled how she'd run from him. That thought sobered him. What was he doing? She'd just shared the details of her tragic past. No doubt, her emotions were all over the place now. There was no way she was thinking clearly.

Sure, she was kissing him enthusiastically now, but later, when her emotions weren't so high, she might regret her actions.

Slowly, he pulled back, ending the kiss. She opened her eyes and looked at him, a quizzical expression on her face. "What's wro g?"

"This is not the right time."

"The right time?"

"It's no secret that I am attracted to you. But today has been emotional for you. And for me too. We're friends. That much is clear. Everything else?" He shrugged. "We need to figure that out. And as much as I want you, I don't want to do anything we might regret later."

She closed her eyes briefly. When she opened them, they glistened with unshed tears. She stroked his cheek gently. "You are a special man, Isaac Montgomery."

Suddenly, he was filled with dread. Why did her words sound like goodbye?

Chapter Seven

I kissed Isaac.

The thought echoed in Savannah's mind as they rode back toward the house. After the kiss, she'd helped Isaac pack up the remains of lunch. Then she'd mounted her horse and ridden beside him to see more of the ranch as if he hadn't just rocked her world. Although her emotions were running the gamut, Isaac was…well, Isaac. He was his normal steady self. His calm demeanor helped her to bring herself under control. It was simply a kiss. No need to make a bigger deal out of it than it was.

In truth, the kiss, although earth-shattering, hadn't been the biggest shock of the day. She hadn't told anyone the details of Darren and Tony's deaths and she'd surprised herself by sharing them with

Isaac. Once she'd begun to talk, the words had spilled from her and she hadn't been able to stop the flow. Hadn't wanted to. His reaction had been exactly what she'd expected from him. Sympathetic. Understanding. Compassionate.

Lying beside him and watching the clouds float overhead, she'd felt better than she had since that horrible day. A weight had been lifted from her shoulders, if only temporarily, leaving her light as air. She hadn't intended for the playful moment to turn romantic. Truthfully, she hadn't expected any of the things that had happened between her and Isaac. Once she'd begun to open up to him, the floodgates had unlocked, leaving her vulnerable to the emotions that had burst from her.

It had been so long since a man's strong arms had enfolded her. Being held by Isaac had felt so good. So perfect. That thought brought her up short and she jerked. That couldn't be right. Only Darren's arms belonged around her. Only his arms felt perfect. Her heart belonged to her husband. Her rogue body needed to get in line.

"We're almost home," Isaac said, pulling her away from her tumultuous thoughts.

"That was quick."

"Going back is always faster. It's the first rule of travel."

She couldn't help but laugh. Isaac had pointed out items of interest on the way to his favorite place, but he'd kept his comments to a minimum on the way back as if knowing she needed quiet time to digest the kiss. "Actually that's the second rule."

"What's the first?"

"The line will be long in front of you and short behind."

He laughed. "True. I hate when that happens."

They kidded each other for the rest of the ride and when they reached the stable, her spirits were high once more. They dismounted and Savannah was pleased that she had been able to get off the horse on her own.

"Are you okay? Stiff? Wobbly legs?" Isaac asked as he removed the saddle and blanket from Samson's back.

She took two cautious steps away from Wildfire and then walked back. "Nope. I'm fine."

She removed the saddle and blanket as she'd seen Isaac do.

"I can take care of your horse."

"No way. I rode her so I'm going to be responsible for her. Just show me what I need to do."

From the expression on his face, Savannah knew she'd said the right thing. Not that she was trying to impress him. Much.

"Okay." He showed her how to check Wildfire's hooves for pebbles. When she was done, he handed her a brush and demonstrated how to groom the horse. The motion was soothing, and Wildfire seemed to enjoy her attention. When they were finished, they gave the horses water and hay.

Savannah and Isaac washed their hands and then took the path back to the patio.

"It looks like Miles and Jillian stopped by," Isaac said as they grew nearer to the house. "You met Miles the other day. Do you want to meet his fiancée?"

Before Savannah could respond, Miles waved. He said something to the woman sitting beside him and she waved too.

"Sure."

When they reached them, Isaac took Savannah's hand as if knowing that she could use a bit of support. She wasn't by nature a shy person, but she'd gotten out of the habit of interacting with people.

"Miles, you remember Savannah," Isaac said.

"Of course. It's good to see you again."

"You too," Savannah said.

Miles put his arm around a stunning woman and pulled her to his side. "This is my fiancée, Jillian."

"It's nice to meet you," Jillian said. "How did you enjoy your ride?"

"It was nice," Savannah replied honestly. "I enjoyed seeing the ranch and getting some fresh air."

"If you enjoy outside activities, you should definitely stop by my parents' resort. We have fun things to do all year round. At this time of year, you can hike, bike and fish, to name just a few things." Jillian grinned mischievously. "If you think the ranch is beautiful, wait until you see our resort. It'll knock your socks off, as my dad likes to say."

"Did you just insult our ranch?" Isaac asked.

Jillian grinned. "I'm just telling it the way it is."

Isaac glanced over at his brother. "Are you going to just stand there grinning while she talks trash?"

"Happy wife, happy life."

Isaac shook his head. He pulled out a chair for Savannah and then sat down beside her.

"Are you saying the resort isn't beautiful?" Jillian challenged.

"Of course not."

"Case closed," Jillian said. She winked at Savannah. "You can have Isaac bring you over anytime. It's not far from here. If you'd rather have girl time, give me a call and we can get together. Isaac has my number."

"Thanks," Savannah said. Jillian was friendly and Savannah liked her instantly. From the way she and Isaac teased each other, it was clear that they were good friends.

"We need to get going," Jillian said after a while. "I'll go get Benji and Lilliana."

"We need to get going too," Isaac said, jumping to his feet and standing behind Savannah's chair. He gave it a yank and she stood. "Give Lilliana and Benji a kiss for me. Tell Mom I'll be back for Mia in a little while."

Jillian gave him a perplexed look. "Okay. It was nice meeting you, Savannah."

"You too."

Savannah walked beside Isaac to his SUV. When they were inside, she turned and looked over at him. "What was that about?"

"What?"

"You rushed me out of there real fast."

He inhaled and then slowly blew out the breath. "I know. I was trying to be considerate of you. Maybe I was wrong, and if I was, I apologize."

"Considerate how?"

"Miles has a three-year-old son and Jillian has a two-year-old daughter. After dredging up those painful memories of your son and husband, I wasn't sure how you would feel about being around children that age."

"Oh." Relief coursed through her. Isaac was one of a kind. At another place or time, she would have thought he was a keeper. But in the here and now, she knew she should keep her distance before she did something scary—like fall for him.

"Was I wrong?"

"No. I avoid being around children, especially little boys, whenever possible. I know that it's not entirely rational, but there it is. That's my truth. And today was especially emotional for me, so thank you."

"Of course. If there is anything I can do to help, you only need to say the word."

"You already did."

They rode in companionable silence the rest of the short distance to her cabin. Isaac helped her from the SUV and they walked together to her front door. As they drew nearer, her heart began to pound. Would he try to kiss her? Did she want him to? The guilt and longing battling inside her supported her belief that she was not ready for a romantic relationship. Even with Isaac.

He was a good man. A stellar man. The type of man a woman could build a family with. But she'd had one family and wasn't considering having another. She didn't have it within her to open her heart to him or his child.

So what was she doing with him?

"I had a good time," Isaac said. "Thanks for sharing part of your day with me."

"I really enjoyed myself," she said honestly.

"I meant what I said about feeling free to ride. You're welcome anytime at all. Just give me a call and I'll have a horse ready for you. And, of course, if you want company, I'm your man."

"Thank you." Scout must have heard them talking because he barked. Savannah heard his steps moments before he pressed his nose to the window. "I should let him out."

He nodded. After a moment, he leaned down and kissed her. His lips were gentle as they met hers, yet she felt herself begin to melt like ice cream sitting in the sun. And then he ended the kiss, leaving her hungry for more. "If it's okay with you, I'll call you later."

She nodded, as if she hadn't just decided that he deserved more than she could give him. "That would be nice."

"I'll talk to you later, then, Savannah." He tapped her nose with the tip of his finger before jogging down the stairs. She was still trying to figure out what was going on inside her when he honked the horn once and drove off. It was only after he'd vanished from sight that she stepped inside. Scout ran over to greet her. Savannah knelt down and gave him a big hug. "I'm home now. Let's grab a leash so you can go out."

As they walked around the yard, Savannah made a mental note to buy a wireless fence. That way, Scout could run free without straying too far. While Scout sniffed around, Savannah's mind replayed the kisses she'd shared with Isaac. She knew she should stay away from him for both of their sakes. So why was it so hard to do?

As Isaac drove back to the ranch, his mind kept wandering to Savannah. Actually, it didn't so much stray as it raced. His mind replayed every minute they'd spent together. He couldn't remember the last time he'd had this much fun with a woman while wearing clothes. She was funny, with a clever mind. He admired her quick wit and quirky sense of humor, on those occasions it peeked out.

It was thrilling to be with someone who appreciated his intellect as much as his ability to party with the best of them.

He was ready for a change. He wanted a relationship with a woman with depth. A woman he could talk to about his hopes and dreams for the future. He also wanted a physical relationship with Savannah. This afternoon he'd wanted nothing more than to make love with her on the soft bed of grass. He'd known she was willing, but she'd also been vulnerable. And he couldn't take advantage of that vulnerability.

Jillian and Miles were gone when he returned to the ranch. His mother had Mia on her lap and was spooning mushy peas and some brown gunk into the baby's mouth. It all looked terrible, but Mia kept opening her mouth whenever the spoon came near, so she must like it.

He pulled out a chair and reached for the baby. "I can feed her if you want."

"She's just about done."

"I don't see how she eats that stuff. It's n-a-s-t-y."

Michelle laughed. "You say that now. You used to eat it. All of you did."

"I don't remember that."

"You were a baby. And it's baby food."

"It was probably so traumatic that I blanked it out."

His parents laughed.

"I like Savannah," his father said. "She's nice."

"And not at all your usual type," Michelle added and then gave Mia a sippy cup, which she drained in a minute. Michelle wiped Mia's mouth with the bib that dangled across the baby's chest, unsnapped it, then stood and placed her in the playpen. Mia instantly began pounding on a toy piano.

"What does that mean?"

"Don't get all huffy. It wasn't a criticism. Just an observation. You tend to date…you know. Flashier women. Lots of makeup, the latest fashions—"

Criticism or not, Miles felt compelled to cut off his mother and defend Savannah. "Savannah doesn't need all of those things to be appealing."

"I know. And I'm not putting her down, nor the women you usually date. I'm the first to believe a woman should do what she wants with her body."

"So do I."

She smiled and patted his cheek. "I know. That's because we raised you right."

"But you like her?" Isaac asked. He admired his parents and wanted them to approve of his choice. More than that, he knew they were good judges of character.

"Yes," his parents said in unison.

Happy with that response, Isaac stood. "I need

to get Mia home for her nap. She'll be a lot more comfortable in her crib than in her playpen. Thanks again for watching her."

"You know I love having a little girl to spoil."

"That's because you're the best." Isaac kissed his mother's cheek.

"Hey, I like spoiling her too," Edward added.

"You're the best too." Isaac kissed his dad's cheek.

"You'd better recognize," Edward said, laughing.

Isaac picked up Mia. Even after all this time, he was still surprised by how light she felt in his arms. Weren't babies supposed to be chubby?

His mother had assured him that she weighed enough for her age, but he'd taken her to the pediatrician anyway. The doctor had said the same thing as Michelle, but Isaac had only been slightly comforted. Perhaps if she had something good to eat as opposed to jars of meat that stunk to high heaven and mashed carrots, she'd put some meat on her bones. When he'd said that, the doctor had written down a list of books for Isaac to read. He was now in the middle of *What to Expect the First Year*. It had cut down on his fear, but he had a suspicion that an undercurrent of worry would be his constant companion for the rest of his life.

Mia squirmed around, making herself comfortable on his chest. When she found a spot she liked, she sighed and popped her thumb into her mouth.

Love overflowed his heart. He'd do anything for his little girl. They might not be related by blood, but she was his daughter. Love mattered. Not biology.

"Are you coming for dinner tomorrow?" Michelle asked.

"Not sure. I'll play it by ear." He headed for his SUV.

When they got home, Isaac changed Mia's diaper and then lay her in the crib so she could take a nap. He wanted to call Savannah, if only to hear her voice, but decided against it. He didn't want to pressure her. Given everything she'd been through, pressure was the last thing she needed from him. What she needed was space. So no matter how much it pained him, he was going to give it to her.

Chapter Eight

"A watched phone never rings," Savannah said to herself that night. She'd kept her cell phone nearby all day and knew it hadn't rung. She knew she was being utterly ridiculous—after all, she had Isaac's number, so she didn't have to wait for him to call. She could call him. But she'd made up her mind that there was no future for them, so why encourage him?

Leading him on would be cruel. She didn't want a relationship. A fling would be okay, but he didn't seem the type for casual connections. He struck her as someone looking for a lifetime commitment.

Scout barked and ran to the back door. They'd just come inside five minutes ago, so Savannah knew he wasn't hearing the call of nature. The dog was just bored. Savannah couldn't just let Scout out on his own, especially at this time of night. There was only one thing to do. She needed to buy the wireless fence the vet had told her about. Since she wasn't sleepy and she was driving herself up a wall, she might as well go into town and get it now. She could set it up in the morning and Scout could have as much outside time as he wanted from then on.

When Savannah grabbed her keys and purse, Scout raced over to her and sat on his haunches. "Sorry, pal. You aren't going with me. But I'm getting something just for you."

Scout whined and then ran over to his bed and began gnawing on a chew toy. Feeling guiltier than any human in her situation should, Savannah closed the door and headed to her car. As she drove down the highway to the big box store, she thought of the other times she'd run into Isaac at the store.

She hadn't expected to see him here tonight, but she looked around as she stood at the checkout and felt a bit disappointed when she didn't.

Savannah loaded the wireless fence system in the trunk of her car and just stood there. She didn't feel like going back home right now. There was nothing waiting for her there except Scout, who would be fine with chew toys, and a cell phone that wouldn't ring. With nothing better to do, she headed for Main Street. It was deserted, so she easily found a parking space.

She got out of her car and strolled down the deserted walk. The streetlights were shining brightly, and the moon and stars provided additional illumination. Although she couldn't make out the colors of the flowers in the beds, she easily made out their shapes. The wind blew gently, scenting the air with sweet perfume. The trees lining the streets swayed, and their leaves rustled softly. It was nice. Peaceful.

It was an unseasonably warm night, and she was perfectly comfortable in her maxi dress and denim jacket. She was in no particular hurry, so she decided to wander through town. Music spilled from a club to her right, so went to the left. The stores had long since closed, but their displays were illuminated, perfect for window shopping. Not that she was looking to buy any of the fancy clothes. She didn't have any social engagements on her calendar so they would languish unworn in her closet. Even so, she admired the garments in the boutiques.

Every time she'd encountered Isaac, she'd been dressed casually. Her clothes, although of good quality, weren't especially memorable or noteworthy. Serviceable had become her mantra. Now, though, she found herself imagining what she'd look like in one of those fashionable outfits.

She heard a baby's voice behind her and turned. Isaac was standing at a distance. Now that she'd spotted him, he started in her direction. Mia was in her stroller, shaking a rattle and…singing? Although her heart stuttered, the slight pang immediately vanished. Savannah was charmed by the little girl.

"Hi," Isaac said, closing the distance between them. Her stomach did the familiar flip-flop thing it did whenever he was around.

"Hi, yourself." She brushed a hand over her hair to be sure it was neat. "What are you doing here at this time of night?"

"I nodded off while Mia was taking a nap. Consequently, she slept way too long. Now she's wide-awake. Everyone swears that riding in a car puts babies to sleep, so I thought I'd drive to town and back home. When I got to Aspen Creek, she was still pretending to be a percussionist, so I decided that we may as well walk around while we're here."

"How long did she nap?"

"Oh, about four hours."

Savannah laughed. "That's not a nap. That's a sleep."

"I didn't intend for either of us to sleep that long. I actually fell asleep in a chair. I got her up the second I woke up."

He looked so flustered that she couldn't help but smile.

"So what's your excuse?" Isaac asked. They'd begun strolling side by side down the street, as if meeting up in the middle of the night for a stroll was normal.

Savannah shrugged. "Shopping. I bought one of

those wireless fences for Scout. That way he'll be able to go outside whenever he wants and I won't have to worry about him getting lost."

"Good thinking."

"I thought so. It's such a nice night, so I decided to walk around town."

"You do that a lot."

"I guess. Why waste all of this beauty when it's in your backyard?"

He nodded. Of course, he could have pointed out that she actually had even more beauty in her literal backyard, but he didn't.

They walked in silence for a few more minutes, but neither of them seemed compelled to fill it with unnecessary words.

After a while, they ended up in the park. By silent agreement, they stepped onto the grass and began heading for the playground.

When they reached the swings, Isaac settled Mia into a baby swing, belting her in securely in the bucket seat before giving the swing a gentle push. It moved about an inch. Mia jiggled the swing then laughed and kicked her feet, a sign that she wanted to go faster. Ah, a girl after Savannah's own heart. No meek gliding for her. Mia jerked her body and then spun around to look at Isaac. She spit out a few syllables as she stared at him.

"You want to get out?" Isaac asked. It was indisputable that he loved his little girl, but he clearly didn't understand what she was saying.

"No. That's not what she wants at all. She wants to swing higher and faster," Savannah said.

"Higher?" Isaac sounded positively weak at the idea.

"And faster."

"I don't know. Is that really safe?"

"I'm not talking about sending her super high. The swing won't even allow that. Just a little bit more motion so that she's actually moving."

Mia had begun to fuss so, naturally, Isaac reached for her. Savannah knocked her hip into his, moving him out of the way. In the same motion, she grabbed the chains and lifted the swing a little and then let go. It sailed for about a foot. Mia instantly squealed and clapped her hands.

"She likes it," Isaac said, his voice filled with confusion.

"Well, I told you. She may be a baby, but she has her own idea of what's fun."

"Swinging fast and high."

"It's actually not that fast or high," Savannah pointed out. She seriously hoped he didn't panic and scare the baby.

He sucked in a deep breath and his massive chest expanded. She wouldn't be surprised if a button or two popped under the strain. Slowly, he let the breath out and his mouth lifted in a sheepish grin. "Sorry for freaking out on you like that."

"I get it. You're a new dad and you're worried about Mia."

"Every second of every day."

She could have told him that worrying was a waste of time. She and Darren had worried about everything. They'd babyproofed their house and car. Didn't let anyone near Tony who might have had a cold. Watched like a hawk as he ate, played and slept. And it had all been for nothing. Tony had been snatched away in the blink of an eye.

Rather than answer, which might lead to a conversation she didn't have the energy or the heart to have, she sat down in the swing next to Mia's. The grass beneath the swings had been worn away, leaving only hard dirt behind. Leaning back, she pushed off and began to swing. She felt Isaac's eyes on her as she sailed through the air. She did her best to ignore him and tried to grab hold of the peace that was always just out of reach.

Being around Mia dragged memories that Savannah had shoved into the recesses of her mind to the forefront. Seeing that sweet baby kicking her legs as she delighted in the motion of the swing only served as a reminder of all that Savannah had lost.

It wasn't as if Savannah wanted to forget her son. She absolutely didn't. Her little boy was etched on her soul and would always be a part of her. But she wanted to remember him without pain or tears. So far, that had proved difficult. Even now, the pain threatened to overcome her, but she clamped down on it, focusing instead on the breeze blowing through her hair.

The swing beside her moved and she glanced over. Isaac was sitting down beside her, holding Mia securely on his lap. She and Isaac swung in silence for a while. Then he grabbed his phone from his pocket and tapped a few buttons. In a minute, music filled the air.

Isaac hummed the song's introduction then began to sing along with the words. She really liked his voice and she listened, transfixed, as he sang a song promising a night of ecstasy followed by a lifetime of happiness. She didn't think a lifetime of happiness was in the cards for her, but she was not opposed to a night of ecstasy. Her heart might be walled off, but her libido was suddenly letting her know it was alive and kicking. She knew Isaac—his kindness, his understanding—was the impetus for that. Something about him rang all of her bells. She'd tried hard to ignore the tolling, but she was growing weary of fighting the attraction.

Closing her eyes, she let herself be carried away by the cadence of his voice, the freedom that came from sailing through the air, and the cool evening breeze blowing over her body.

The song ended and was quickly followed by

another ballad. Her swing came to a sudden halt and she opened her eyes. Mia had fallen asleep and Isaac had set her in the stroller. He was standing beside her, the chains in his hands. "Dance with me."

He released the chains and held out his hands. Savannah smiled and rose, and then stepped closer to him. She inhaled deeply and was treated to his enticing masculine scent. He smelled so good, like outside and spice. Like peace. They began to move to the beat, dancing together as if they'd done it many times over the years as opposed to this being their first time.

As they moved together, a sense of calm filled Savannah that was unlike anything she'd felt in four hundred and forty-seven days. She snuggled closer and Isaac began to caress her back. Being held in his arms was heavenly and she sighed in bliss. Before she could think better of it, she lifted her face to his. He must have shared her yearning because he lowered his head and brushed his lips across hers. She didn't want another sweet kiss that would leave her unsatisfied. She wanted one filled with heat and passion to match the fire burning inside her.

She wrapped her arms around his neck and opened her mouth to him. His tongue swept inside and began dancing with hers. Her knees weakened and she clung to his shoulders. Heat shot through her, sending her up in flames. The intensity of her desire shocked her.

This was wrong. She shouldn't be reacting like this with Isaac. With any man. It was ridiculous to think that way, but she felt like she was being unfaithful to Darren.

She was pulling away just as Mia let out a cry. Isaac stepped back at the same time as Savannah. She swiped a hand across her mouth in a futile attempt to erase what she'd done, yet Isaac's taste lingered.

"What's wrong, baby?"

Mia continued to cry. Isaac picked her up and then reached for the diaper bag that he'd placed on the ground. He tried to unzip the bag, but he couldn't do it with only one hand. The more he struggled, the more flustered he became. And the harder Mia cried.

Mia stretched her arms out to Savannah, her tearstained face a portrait of beseeching.

"No," Isaac said, turning the baby away.

"I can hold her for a moment," Savannah said, surprising herself. Listening to Mia cry was breaking her heart.

"Are you sure?"

"Yes."

Savannah took the little girl into her arms. Immediately, Mia leaned her head against Savannah's breasts, her face hidden from Savannah's eyes. Mia blew out a breath and her sobs slowed. Instinctively,

Savannah rubbed Mia's back and swayed from side to side as she cooed to the baby.

Mia didn't weigh much, but holding her had an outsized impact on Savannah. So many emotions raced through her. Grief. Wonder. Sorrow. Longing. Not just for Tony, but for the opportunity to rock Mia to sleep. Longing to hold the little girl for more than these brief moments, inhaling that familiar sweet baby smell. That thought ricocheted through her, rocking her to her core.

I need to get away from here. Now.

"Thanks," Isaac said. He took Mia from Savannah and handed the baby a pacifier. She popped it into her mouth and snuggled into Isaac's chest, flashing a happy smile at Savannah.

Suddenly, Savannah's arms felt empty—as empty as they'd felt when she'd accepted that she would never hold Tony again—and she yearned to take Mia into her arms once more.

"What's wrong?"

"What do you mean?"

"You're crying."

Savannah touched her cheek, surprised by the moisture she felt there. "I need to go."

Isaac nodded, understanding without an explanation. "I'll walk you to your car."

"That's not necessary," Savannah said, backing away. "You have your hands full. I'll see you later."

Savannah turned and walked away before Isaac

could protest. She knew that she should have kept him at a distance. Why hadn't she?

Isaac watched as Savannah hurried across the park. He grabbed his belongings and followed, keeping her in his sight. She shouldn't be behind the wheel of a car in her frame of mind. The last thing she needed was to be in an accident.

He thought of how he'd put her in this position. She'd told him how much it hurt to be around children. That was why he'd decided to give her some space so she could deal with the feelings she'd dredged up today. He hadn't let one full day pass before approaching her. True, he hadn't expected to run into her tonight and he could have sauntered off before she'd seen him.

But he hadn't. Instead, he'd stood there, staring at her, taking her in from head to toe. She'd looked just as beautiful as she'd been that morning. She'd changed out of the jeans she'd worn earlier and was wearing a colorful dress that floated around her ankles. Her curly hair was free and drifted around her shoulders.

He'd been mesmerized and powerless to look away. He'd been so quiet that she hadn't known he was there. When Mia had become bored, shaken her rattle and babbled at him, the jig was up.

When Savannah had turned to look at them, he'd been spellbound by her beauty. Captivated by the light in her eyes and the delighted smile on her face. Nothing in the world could have convinced him to stick with his original plan to keep his distance.

Things had been going well until he'd touched her. Once he'd held her in his arms, all of his best intentions had gone up in flames—as had he. There was no way they would part without kissing.

He shook his head in an attempt to rid himself of the images of them together. Right now, Savannah was upset. Hurt. Because of him.

Isaac placed Mia in her car seat, loaded the stroller, then got in behind the wheel. There was no way he would be able to rest tonight until he knew that Savannah had made it home safely. At this time of night, there was very little traffic, so he didn't worry about her colliding with another vehicle. But there was plenty of wildlife that could cross the highway at the wrong time. Every once in a while, there had been accidents or near misses with deer crossing the road.

"We're going by Savannah's," Isaac said to Mia, who only looked at him as she gnawed on her pacifier. "I'm glad you have no complaints. And it would be good if you decided to sleep at night again."

She laughed.

Isaac game-planned as he drove. He would check to ensure that Savannah's car was in the driveway. After all, his concern was her getting home safely.

When he reached the cabin and saw her parked

car, he intended to drive away. Then he'd seen a lamp burning in the front window. She was awake.

Was she still upset? Crying? The idea tore his heart and he knew he couldn't drive home without knowing whether she was still distressed. That was callous.

"Looks like we're going inside."

Mia pulled the pacifier out of her mouth and waved it as Isaac as she babbled a few words. Was she lecturing him or giving him encouragement? And when did he start taking advice from ten-month-olds?

He released Mia from her car seat and climbed the stairs. One second after he knocked on the door, he realized his error. Seeing Mia had upset Savannah the first time. Bringing them face-to-face again was stupid. Heartless.

The door swung open to reveal Savannah standing there.

"I'm sorry. I just wanted to make sure that you got home okay. Now that I know, I'll leave. Good night."

"You don't have to leave." Savannah stepped aside, letting him inside.

"Are you sure?"

"Have a seat."

He walked through the immaculate room and sat on the couch. There was a framed photo on the side table, and he picked it up. Savannah was standing beside a handsome man, a toddler between them. A stadium was in the background. "Your family?"

"Yes. We took that picture at a UW Madison home football game. Darren played in college and he wanted Tony to develop a love of the game."

"Did Tony like it?"

"He liked the junk food. He wasn't a fan of all the noise, though. We left at halftime, which Darren thought was criminal. I don't think he ever left a game with time still on the clock in his life. Even if the game was a blowout."

"He sounds like a fun guy and a good father."

"He was the best. They both were."

"I'm sorry you lost them."

"I didn't lose them. They were stolen from me." Her voice was fierce. Angry. "I'm sorry. I shouldn't have snapped at you."

"Don't apologize for how you feel."

She nodded. "Thank you for that. And for not telling me to try to find a way to make peace with what happened. To get over it."

"Is that even possible?"

"That's what everyone kept telling me. Friends. Family. Coworkers. At first, it hurt me. Then it made me angry. I felt as if they were telling me that my husband and sweet baby were only deserving of so much sorrow. Like there was a quota of days and I'd exceeded it. That it was time for me to pick up the shreds of my life and start living again. I know they meant well, that it hurt them to see me so sad, but still…" She frowned as her voice faded away.

He understood how her friends and family had felt. Witnessing her obvious pain was like having a knife shoved into his gut. And then twisted. But he knew nothing he felt compared to what Savannah was feeling. "I'm sorry that happened to you."

"You aren't going to tell me that they meant well?"

"No."

She looked at him as if he were a space alien. "Why not? Everyone else does."

"Because their intent doesn't matter. What matters is the effect. They hurt and disappointed you. You're entitled to be angry. I would be."

She chuckled, but it didn't hold any mirth. "I was reluctant to let you into my life, but now I have to admit I'm glad to have your friendship."

He was coming to want more than that, but friendship would work for now. "I'm glad that we're friends too."

She sat there silently, staring at her hands. Mia yawned loudly.

"I guess that's my sign." He rose. "I need to get this little one to bed. And I could use a bit of sleep myself."

She stood and walked with him to the door. "Thanks for checking on me."

He nodded. Although he was glad to see that she had made it home safely, he was concerned about her state of mind. He'd thought she was working through her grief, but she was clearly in so much pain. And there was nothing he could do to change that.

Chapter Nine

Savannah stood outside the boutique, staring at the lovely dresses in the window. Judging from the display, the store sold some absolutely gorgeous clothes that she would love to own. But where would she wear them? Tromping through the woods behind the cabin?

How about on a date with Isaac?

The thought came from out of nowhere. It was so ridiculous that it wasn't worthy of a second thought.

She hadn't spoken with him since they'd run into each other Sunday night. Five days ago. Perhaps he'd come to the same conclusion that she had. They'd crossed a line and needed to take a step back before they made a huge mistake.

"Excuse me," a woman said, and Savannah realized she had drifted from the window and was now blocking the door to the boutique that two women were waiting to enter.

"I'm sorry," Savannah said. She pulled open the door and stepped inside with the women.

"No worries," the taller one said. "It happens to the best of us."

"I get mesmerized all of the time just looking at all of the beautiful clothes," the shorter one said, waving an arm, encompassing the entire shop. She smiled and walked off with her friend.

Savannah looked around. The boutique was larger than it appeared from the outside. She tried to figure out where to begin. She hadn't intended to come inside, and she definitely hadn't planned to buy anything, but now that she was here...

It had been years since she'd bought clothes and she suddenly found herself picking up items with no rhyme or reason. If it caught her eye—and a great deal did—she grabbed it. Before long, her arms overflowed with an assortment of summer clothes. She'd selected three dresses that had initially appealed to her as well as two additional cute little numbers. She knew that she wouldn't be able to wear all of the clothes in her arms, yet she kept shuffling through the hangers, adding more.

"I can start a fitting room for you, if you want." Savannah turned and looked into the smiling face of a young, impeccably dressed woman. "I'm not going to get all of these."

"Trying them on isn't a commitment." Her eyes sparkled with humor as she held out her arms.

"I'm still looking," Savannah said as she handed over the clothes.

"Take your time. I'm Marissa. If you need anything, just let me know and I'll help you."

"It's just that everything here is so beautiful that it's hard to choose," Savannah said with a sigh.

"I know what you mean. I swear that I spend half of my check here."

"I can see how that would happen."

Marissa and Savannah shared a smile.

As Marissa walked toward the changing rooms, Savannah turned her attention back to the racks and, within twenty minutes, she'd filled her arms again.

Unable to hold one more thing, she headed for the dressing room. Once inside, she stood there, looking at the clothes. Wow. What had possessed her to grab so many things? Reminding herself that there was no harm in trying them on, she stripped out of her jeans and blouse and pulled on the dress that had drawn her eyes. The silky fabric felt so good against her skin; a welcome change to the cotton and denim she'd been wearing.

There was a mirror attached to the wall, and she studied her reflection. The neckline dipped in a V and the skirt skimmed her hips. Savannah wanted to see the dress from all angles, so she stepped into the corridor and headed for the three-way mirror at the end of the changing area. The two women she'd encountered earlier were taking turns checking their appearance in front of the mirror. The taller one looked at Savannah and gave a thumbs-up.

"Wow. That's a keeper," the other woman said. She'd been checking her reflection, but now she stopped to give Savannah her opinion.

"Thanks. I have absolutely nowhere to wear it."

"Once you see how good you look, you'll think of somewhere." She stepped aside, giving Savannah access to the mirrors.

"It's not too dressy," the first woman said. "You can wear that every day. To work. To lunch. Or just around town. If you want to dress it down, wear cowboy boots. If you want to dress it up, you can wear high-heeled sandals or pumps. Silver jewelry will totally work with the blue and white."

"Thanks. You're right." In that moment, she missed her girlfriends. They'd always gone shopping together and she could count on their honest critiques. She'd been confident knowing that they wouldn't let her buy anything that didn't accentuate her best attributes.

"No problem. Now, what do you think about the outfit Janice has on? I can't decide if I like it or not."

Savannah looked at the shorter woman, whom she presumed was Janice. The style was perfect for her shape, but there was something about the green that didn't work with the other woman's complexion. Not wanting to be rude, but not wanting to let the other woman spend money on something she might regret buying, Savannah decided to be honest and diplomatic all at once. "The fit is great. Does it come in another color? I think you would look great in coral or peach."

The taller woman crowed triumphantly. "That's what I said."

"I know, Tiffany. But I always wear those colors. I wanted to try something different."

"That's because they look great on you."

"You know, you can always get a peach top and then wear a floral skirt with green in it. I have one in my dressing room I can show you."

"Okay."

Savannah dashed to her room, grabbed the skirt off the hanger, and returned to the other woman. It was mostly green, but it had pops of coral and peach. "You can still wear green all the while wearing the color that suits you best."

Janice held the skirt up to her. "I do like this. I'll see if they have my size. Thanks."

"You're welcome. And thanks for your opinion on this dress."

Savannah returned to her dressing room and traded in the dress for a pair of pants and a coordinating top. When she stepped up to the mirror, Janice had changed into the other outfit. "That looks great on you."

"Thanks."

"My name is Savannah, by the way."

"Nice to meet you."

They continued to comment on each other's clothes. Savannah found herself laughing and she realized that she missed Cheris, her best friend. She'd cut off all contact with her when Cheris had suggested that it might do Savannah good to go out to lunch with her friends. At the time, she'd been so buried by her pain that she'd been unable to understand her friend had only been trying to help keep Savannah from spiraling into depression. That she'd been coming from a place of love.

Savannah made a vow to contact Cheris and apologize. If possible, she'd try to rebuild the friendship they'd had since seventh grade.

Janice and Tiffany had finished trying on their outfits and were now waiting for Savannah to come out wearing her last one. As she approached them in a daring black dress that she'd grabbed on impulse, she heard them talking.

"I hope he shows up this weekend. I can really use a good time," Tiffany said.

"He hasn't been to the clubs in ages. I'm wondering if he did something crazy like elope. Or worse, maybe he got religion and no longer parties."

Tiffany laughed and then turned to look at Savannah. "That is a keeper. You look really sexy. Maybe too sexy."

"I love it, but it makes absolutely no sense for me to buy it. I never go anywhere. It would just sit unworn in my closet." Still, she couldn't keep her eyes from straying to her reflection. For one second, her imagination got the best of her and she pictured Isaac's face as he caught a glimpse of her. He wouldn't be able to resist her in this dress. But did she want to be irresistible to him?

Yes.

The whole reason she'd come to town and was currently shopping for a new wardrobe was due to Isaac. She hadn't cared a whit what she'd worn for the past year and a half. It hadn't mattered whether her clothes matched or whether she looked like she was auditioning for a job with the circus.

"You never know what could happen. For all you know, Prince Charming could ring your doorbell some night in desperate need of a date. And where will you be?"

"So you're saying that the only logical thing to do is buy this dress because I might be invited to a ball by a strange man?"

Tiffany shrugged. "It's the best I could do on short notice."

"If you don't run into a prince, you could run into Mr. Love 'em and Leave 'em Happy." Janice and Tiffany looked at each other and laughed.

"Who is that?"

"Aspen Creek's most famous bachelor. Isaac Montgomery. He doesn't do commitment, but when he's with you, he makes you feel like the most important person in the world. You might only get one night, but, baby, that one night is worth it."

Isaac Montgomery? *Her* Isaac? Tiffany continued to talk, but Savannah couldn't make sense of the words. There had to be more than one man with that name. The Isaac Montgomery she knew was nothing like the man they were describing. Sure, he was good-looking and charming, but that was where the similarity ended. But two men named Isaac Montgomery in a town of six thousand? No way. There could only be one. She realized that Janice and Tiffany were waiting for her to respond, so she nodded. "He sounds like he's something else."

"Maybe. But he's honest. To my knowledge, he has never led anyone on. He's always been clear that he's not the marrying kind."

"Besides being a lot of fun, he's a great dancer. And he's good to look at."

"He would have to be," Savannah said.

The clubs are definitely a lot less fun without him."

"Maybe he'll be around this weekend," Janice said.

Savannah glanced at her watch, intending to use the passage of time as an excuse to get out of there. Although she and the other women weren't friends, it still felt icky to not mention that she knew Isaac and why he hadn't been clubbing lately. But it wasn't her business to share. When she saw the time, she couldn't believe it. "Wow. It's later than I thought. I hadn't intended to spend this much time shopping."

"Time flies when you have so many good pieces to choose from," Tiffany said, grabbing the hangers holding her finds.

"It was nice meeting you, Savannah," Janice said.

"You too."

Savannah returned to her dressing room and grabbed the clothes she intended to buy. The pile was larger than she'd expected it to be, but she'd left behind quite a few and couldn't bring herself to part with any of these. Janice and Tiffany were gone by the time Savannah checked out, but what they'd said about Isaac remained.

Had she been wrong about him? She'd thought that he was ready to settle down and raise Mia. A man looking for a serious relationship. Instead, it turns out that he went from woman to woman with no thought of commitment. In another place and time, she would avoid him like the plague.

But this was here and now. And Isaac was sounding like the type of man she needed in her life at the moment. She wasn't looking for a man to build a future with. She'd had that with Darren. At least for a while. She could never replicate what they'd shared, so there was no sense in trying.

Yet, if Isaac wasn't looking for happily-ever-after, she didn't need to keep him at a distance. He wouldn't be hurt by her inability to create a family with him and Mia. Since she didn't have to worry about hurting him, there was no reason to resist the attraction. They could have a fling. And when it ended, they could go their separate ways.

Savannah was so glad she'd bought that sexy dress. More than that, she was happy that she'd talked with Tiffany and Janice. If not for them, she wouldn't know the truth about Isaac. She'd still have the mistaken belief that he was looking for a committed relationship. Now she just needed to figure out how to ask him if he was interested in a fling. The thought of that conversation made her want to run and hide.

She wasn't a prude, but it had been so long since she'd dated anyone. The rules had probably changed. Darren had pursued her, and it hadn't taken her long to let him know that the attraction was mutual. Isaac had done such a good job of being a friend to her that she wasn't sure whether he'd been pursuing her.

Unless he told her otherwise, she was going to believe that Isaac was only interested in having brief flings. She just had to find a way to let him know she wanted the same thing.

She smiled to herself. The best way was always the direct way.

Isaac placed the baby monitor on the patio table, leaned back in the lawn chair and sighed. It had been a long, difficult day, but Mia was finally asleep. Though he had told his mother not to make Mia stay awake all day so she'd sleep at night, he had since seen the wisdom of his mother's way. And so today he'd asked Michelle to keep Mia awake. It was now eight o'clock and Isaac had fed her, given her a bath, and read to her from a Jacqueline Woodson book. Mia was sleeping soundly in her crib and Isaac was pretty sure both he and his daughter would finally get a good night's sleep again.

The night sky was filled with stars and a sweet breeze blew. Perfect weather to spend with a woman; taking a moonlight dip, sharing a bottle of wine, followed by wherever the night led. Although there were many women he could call, there was only one woman he wanted to spend the night with. Savannah. Other women had ceased to exist since the day they'd met.

He hadn't been to a club in a while, and he didn't miss it at all. Well, that wasn't entirely true. There were things that he missed. He missed the energy he felt from being around people; missed hanging out with his friends. He would love to dance and listen to live music again. There was nothing quite like watching a really good band perform in person.

Surprisingly, he didn't miss the women, the flirting, and the attention they showered on him. No woman was without her charms, and he'd always made it his business to find them. Now, though, he wasn't interested in discovering a woman's appeal. He was focused on the one who was stealing his heart. The woman he was falling in love with.

That thought surprised him and he bolted upright, rocking his chair. It was way too early in their relationship to have that kind of idea. Only a fool would mistake sexual magnetism for love. There was no question that he was incredibly attracted to Savannah. Any man would be. She was tall and slender, with the body of a supermodel. Her sexy legs went on forever. Her face was the most beautiful one he'd ever seen. With clear brown skin, high cheekbones and full lips, she was nothing short of stunning.

And her eyes. Though they were often haunted with sorrow, they were intelligent. Kind. On the occasions when he managed to make her laugh, they danced with glee.

Even with his vast experience with women, he was unsure about how to pursue her. He couldn't treat her as any other woman, because she wasn't like others. She'd experienced a loss and grief that very few women had. At times, she seemed to back away from him. At others, she seemed to welcome his attention. But given her history of loss, he understood the battle that was waging inside her. The fear of being hurt fighting against the longing to share life with someone. Tragedy had come to her door once already, snatching away her husband and child. That would be enough to make anyone cautious.

And given his inability—or unwillingness—to commit to a woman in the past, perhaps he should keep his distance. Savannah had been hurt enough in the past. He didn't want to inadvertently add to her pain.

Isaac rubbed a hand down his face. He could stumble around on his own, or he could get advice. He'd ask a woman. Jillian was the closest thing that he had to a sister, so he'd call her.

Isaac was organizing his thoughts when his brother's voice came over the phone. "What are you doing calling my woman?"

Isaac laughed. "I'm checking to see if she's gotten tired of you yet and wants to run away with me."

He heard Miles repeating the message a moment before Jillian's voice came over the line. "Nope. Sorry. I've already chosen my Montgomery man. Besides, we have a date for the wedding and a hall reserved. Not to mention that Lilliana would never forgive me if I took her away from Miles and Benji."

"In that case, I suppose you can stay with Miles." They laughed.

"What can I do for you, Isaac?"

"I want a woman's opinion."

"About?"

"Relationships."

"Oh no, don't tell me it's finally happened. Isaac

Montgomery is in love, and he doesn't know what to do."

"I didn't say I was in love," he said quickly. His brow was suddenly damp and he swiped his arm across it. He didn't want to be in love with Savannah unless she could love him in return. And, of course, there had to be room in her heart for Mia. A huge question mark hung over all of that.

"Well, I doubt you're asking my opinion about someone you don't care about."

"No wonder my brother fell in love with you. You're smart."

"And you're stalling. Are we talking about Savannah?"

"Yes." Isaac quickly told Jillian everything, starting with the night they'd met and ending with their last conversation.

"Wow."

"Yeah. I don't know what to do or how to pursue her."

"And you think I do?"

"I wouldn't have asked you otherwise. You've been through some painful things in your life."

"What I went through is nothing like what Savannah's been through. I was hurt when your brother ended our relationship all those years ago. And I was disappointed that my marriage didn't work out. Neither of those experiences compare to the pain of losing your husband and child. I mean, she moved to an entirely different state to get away from the reminders of what she'd lost."

"You moved away too."

"And I came back."

"Do you think Savannah will go back to Wisconsin?" He sucked in a ragged breath at the thought.

"Is that where she's from?"

"Yes."

"I don't know. I came back because I missed home. Missed my family. I guess the better question to ask is if there's a reason for her to stay here."

"There can be."

"Ah. Sounds like love."

"What should I do? How should I approach her? I don't want to scare her off, but I do want her to know that I'm interested."

"You're not going to like this answer, but I don't have an answer for you. Every woman is different. You know that Savannah has the capacity to love, because she'd loved before. But she's been hurt, so she's understandably wary of giving her heart again. Maybe she won't ever want to take that risk a second time. Or she could want to experience that kind of love again. I don't know. My best advice is to follow your heart."

Isaac groaned. His heart was confused. That was the problem. "I was hoping for a game plan."

"That's what I just gave you. Be honest. Consider her feelings." Jillian paused, but Isaac knew she had more to say so he didn't try to fill the silence. He couldn't think of a response anyway. "You're a good man with good instincts. Trust them."

"Thanks, Jillian. I appreciate your help. Such as it was."

She laughed as he'd intended. "If it matters, Miles and I really liked her."

"I like her too. That's why I don't want to mess up things."

"What's the worst thing that could happen if you make a mistake?"

"I lose her forever."

"That won't happen," Jillian said confidently. "Miles and I made mistakes and we're together."

"True." But that was after they'd each married the wrong person and let years pass before they'd found their way back to each other. He wanted to avoid years of heartache if possible.

They talked a few more minutes before ending the conversation. Jillian was right. He needed to trust his instincts. And they were telling him to call Savannah and let her know that he was interested in a romantic relationship. A committed relationship. He would let her reaction guide him.

Deciding that he'd spent way too much time debating when he'd known all along that he was going to call, he scrolled through his contacts until he saw her name and then pressed the button. He thought he was prepared to talk to her, but when her voice came through his phone, he realized that he had underestimated the effect that she had on him.

When they'd been together, he'd been so focused on her body, her face—*her*—that he hadn't paid much attention to her voice. Now that it was the only connection he had to her, he realized just how sexy it was. Her voice was low. Rich. And at the moment it was filled with rare joy.

"Is now a good time for you to talk?"

"Yes. It's perfect. Scout and I went for a nice walk and then I let him play outside for as long as he wanted. He finally wore himself out. He's in his bed now, chewing on one of his toys, and I'm drinking a nice glass of wine after trying to find something good to watch on television. I have every streaming service known to man, but nothing held my interest. You've just saved me from a night of boredom."

"Uh. You're welcome?"

Savannah laughed. "You know what I meant."

He closed his eyes and tried to picture her. "What kind of shows do you like?"

"It depends on my mood. Right now, I'm enjoying quirky comedies. Throw in a song-and-dance and I'm sold. I also like to watch PBS when they have Broadway musicals or operas on."

"Oh."

"I can tell by that word that you and I don't share tastes."

"I can go for a comedy every now and then. But

Broadway musicals and operas are where I draw the line. Sounds like what to watch when you have insomnia."

"What do you like to watch?"

"I'm not big on TV, to be honest. I would much rather listen to music—not opera, just to be clear—and…"

"And what?"

"Write. I enjoy writing poetry, although I haven't written anything in a while. Nothing good, anyway. And certainly nothing that would impress an English Literature professor like you."

"Don't be so sure. I might like it."

"Or you might think it's cheesy or amateurish, suitable only for wrapping fish."

"I'm not a snob. As long as it conveys what you want to say, then as far as I'm concerned, it's good."

"And if I'm only one step above 'roses are red and violets are blue'?"

"Don't knock it. Consider how many people can recite that rhyme. It has its place. More importantly, it conveys a feeling of love and admiration."

Isaac smiled. It wasn't often that he talked with anyone about his poetry. It was too personal and he was a bit insecure about it. Savannah's positivity was inspiring. "I bet your students loved you."

"They did," she said. Her voice was barely a whisper. "I loved them too. I enjoyed teaching. I loved helping young people—and not-so-young people—see the value and lessons in words written by someone whose life experience differed vastly from theirs. To discover the universal truths there."

"Do you miss it?"

"I miss everything about my old life. But it's gone and I can't get it back."

"You can't get your husband and son back, but you can have other things that made you happy."

"I can't imagine returning to Wisconsin. At least, not to stay. Being there without them was unbearable."

"Are you sure you aren't confusing the pain you felt losing your family with the place?"

"What do you mean?"

"I mean after they died, you would have felt unbearable pain no matter where you were. True, Madison is filled with reminders, but even without them, you would have grieved. Now that your sorrow has diminished, maybe you would feel differently back in Wisconsin."

"Are you trying to get rid of me?" She gave a little laugh, but Isaac wasn't fooled. This was a hard conversation for her.

"Nothing could be further from the truth." The last thing he wanted was for Savannah to leave. But he wouldn't be any kind of friend, and definitely not the man he was raised to be, if he put his wants ahead of her happiness. "But I know how easy it can be to get confused. It takes a lot of work to get your emotions straight."

"I understand that. But I'm certain that I don't want to return to Madison no matter how much I enjoyed teaching. I'll get used to that not being a part of my life."

"You know, there are students in Colorado who would benefit from having you as a professor."

A long silence came over the phone and, as it stretched, he worried that he'd said the wrong thing. He didn't want to pressure her. He'd been trying to help her see that her life still held possibilities.

"This might make me sound foolish, but I hadn't given that a lot of thought."

"That doesn't make you sound foolish. You've suffered a tremendous loss. I imagine getting through the day must be pretty rough."

"Lately, it's been easier. I used to dread getting up, but I've actually started to look forward to a new day. Of course, Scout is up at the crack of dawn and ready to run around, so staying in bed all day is out of the question."

"I hope that dog isn't the only reason you're feeling more optimistic."

"Fishing for a compliment? That doesn't sound like the confident man I've come to know. And it certainly doesn't match your reputation."

"What do you know about my reputation?" That was one of the things he liked about Savannah. She didn't know a thing about him or have preconceived notions. To her, he was simply Isaac Montgomery, the rancher who was learning how to be a father. Not that he was trying to outrun his past. He hadn't done anything wrong. He'd never once deceived a woman. They'd all known he was only interested in a good time.

But that was before Savannah had come into his life. He wasn't certain that he was ready to make a lifetime commitment, but he was leaning in that direction. The idea of having that one special person in his life held a certain appeal. Now that they'd met, he couldn't imagine his life without her.

"Not much. But I heard that you're the love-'em-and-leave-'em type. And from what I heard, nobody was ever disappointed."

"Where did you hear that?" From what he'd seen, Savannah lived an extremely isolated life. To his knowledge, he and his family were the only people she interacted with. In fact, she was this side of being a recluse. Before they'd actually met, he'd caught glimpses of her in town, but always at night and she was always alone.

"At the boutique today."

"The boutique?" There were so many shops in town that it would be impossible to narrow it down to the one that she meant. Not that it mattered.

"Yes. I was shopping for clothes today and I ended up talking with two women who mentioned you and how much you were missed at the clubs. They brought up your reputation."

"You were talking about me?" That was disappointing. He'd thought Savannah was above gossiping. But then, he only knew her as the grieving widow and bereaved mother. Who knew what type of person she'd been before tragedy had struck?

"No. I overheard them discussing you. I didn't mention that I knew you."

"Okay." He felt slightly better, although it felt odd knowing he'd become a topic of discussion. He truthfully didn't think his absence would be noted after all this time. There were plenty of single men in town who also frequented the clubs.

"I'm not the type of person to talk about someone behind their back. Well, I might say something good, but nothing negative or anything that could be misconstrued."

"That's good to know. And, in fairness, I was a fixture at the clubs. But that was all before Mia came into my life."

"Was there someone special in your life before you became Mia's guardian?"

"I'm more than her guardian. I'm her *father*. And no, there was nobody special. I liked to play the field. But I never misled anyone."

"Well…" Her voice trailed off.

"Well, what? Don't you believe me?"

"Of course. I know your character. Besides,

the women only said good things about you. They seemed to genuinely like and miss you."

"Then what were you going to say before you changed your mind?"

She gave an embarrassed laugh. "This is a bit difficult."

"You can tell me anything, Savannah. I hope you know that by now."

"I do." He heard her inhale and then release the breath. "I would like to go out with you."

"Oh."

"I'm not trying to change you. I'm not looking for anything more than you've offered anyone in the past."

"If my reputation has you thinking that I'm—"

"Your reputation is why I'm considering this. I don't think I'll ever be willing to risk my heart again. But I think I'm ready to live again. At least, in some ways."

"What ways?" He didn't know how, but he managed to keep his disappointment out of his voice.

"I'm looking for companionship."

"I can handle that."

"Maybe something more."

"Like what?" He wasn't going to jump to any conclusions. After all, he could be totally misreading the situation.

"Friends with benefits." She let out a nervous

laugh. "I really hate that phrase, but it sums up what I'm looking for."

"You mean a gigolo."

"No. How can you say that? That's not at all what I mean. I like you and I believe you like me."

"You know I do."

"We're attracted to each other. So why not act on that attraction?"

"I'm not opposed to that."

"But please understand that that's all I have to give. I won't want more than a good time. I'm not going to fall in love with you. And I don't expect you to fall in love with me. In fact, if I hadn't learned of your reputation and your ability to separate the physical from the emotional, I wouldn't be making this proposition. It's important that you know that these terms are nonnegotiable."

The disappointment returned. That was the last thing he'd expected to hear. "Women often say that they can keep things separate. And they do until they don't. How do I know that you won't fall in love with me? And how can you be sure I won't fall in love with you?"

"That's easy. I don't have it in me to love again. Not now. Not ever."

"Don't say that, Savannah. You never know what the future holds."

"Maybe not, but I know what I'm capable of. And what I'm not. What I have to lose."

"But what if you don't lose? What if you love and the two of you live a long, long time and are extremely happy? What if you have a child who is healthy and also lives a long, long life? You're letting fear cheat you out of possible joy."

"I hear what you're saying, and it sounds perfectly logical. And I know it's coming from a good place. But it's not a risk I'm willing to take. You're a good man and the last thing I want to do is cause you pain." She hesitated. "Do you think you might start to love me? If so, we can stop before we start. Go back to the way things were. The last thing I want to do is hurt you."

"Don't worry about that," he said. "After all, my reputation precedes me."

He'd been intent on changing his ways, becoming a different type of man. But if the only way to be a part of Savannah's life was to agree to her plan, then he would.

Savannah's voice was soft. "So…just to be clear. Are you interested in what I'm offering? Will that be enough for you, knowing I will never let myself love you?"

Chapter Ten

Savannah held her breath as she waited for Isaac's response. She couldn't believe that she'd actually had the nerve to proposition him. According to Tiffany and Janice, this type of casual relationship was right up his alley. But what if they'd been exaggerating matters? Or what if he'd once been free and easy with his affection, but he'd changed since Mia had come into his life? Given the up-and-down nature of their relationship, and the way Savannah had run hot and cold, he was probably confused. She hoped she hadn't offended him. After all, she liked him and would hate to lose his friendship.

Unless she'd just stepped over a line…?

Before she could tell him to forget the whole thing, he answered. "Okay. I can handle that."

A breath whooshed out of her, and she realized just how desperately she'd wanted him to agree. "Good. So what do we do now?"

He chuckled. It was a low sound that stirred up something in her stomach. She tried to squash it, but she was only partially successful. Then she reminded herself that it was fine to desire him. As long as her heart didn't try to join the act.

"You mean you haven't worked that out yet?"

"No. I wasn't sure you would agree."

"You can't be serious. You're a beautiful, sexy woman. No man in his right ~~man~~ would turn down what you're offering." *MIND*

He sounded strange, as if he were being ironic. But why? Perhaps he was a bit unsure of how to act. After all, her proposal had come out of the blue. "Okay."

"How about we go to dinner? Jillian's brother, Marty, owns a restaurant in town. The food is top tier. Reservations are hard to get, but since his sister is marrying my brother, we're practically family."

"I wasn't expecting that."

"Wasn't expecting what?"

"Dinner."

"Why? Did you expect me to race over there and drag you into bed?"

"No. And dragging wouldn't be necessary." She'd been trying to add a little levity to the conversation, but she'd failed miserably. All of these months of avoiding people had stripped her of her previously sharp social skills. At this rate, she hoped that she still remembered how to behave in a ritzy restaurant.

"Noted. Now, about dinner? Does tomorrow night work for you?"

"Saturday's a date night."

A heavy sigh came over the phone. "Savannah, we're still friends. Right? I mean friends with benefits assumes that there is a friendship there. Correct?"

"Yes."

"Then as my friend, I would like to take you to dinner tomorrow. And if you know how, I would like to take you dancing afterward."

"What do you mean *if I know how*?"

"As you've told me many times, you're from a college town. When I hear college town, I think a date is pizza and a pitcher of beer. Maybe a tailgate or two before the football game."

She'd eaten her fair share of pizza and toasted victories with beer, but she wasn't going to admit that now. Not when he'd made it sound so provincial. "That doesn't mean I can't dance, cowboy. I can. You just be careful not to step on my dancing shoes with your cowboy boots."

He laughed, and this time it wasn't the least bit ironic, and she breathed a sigh of relief. They had hit a rough patch where they'd had difficulty communicating, but they had navigated their way through it. Thankfully, they were on solid ground again. She was glad because she really liked Isaac and didn't want to hurt him.

They firmed up the details of their date before ending the conversation.

When Savannah hung up, she twirled around the room like a ballerina. *She'd done it.* She'd actually changed the terms of their relationship. And Isaac had said yes. She'd never had a friends-with-benefits relationship before, so she didn't know the rules. Lucky for her, Isaac did. If even half of what she'd heard about him was true, he might have even written a few of them himself.

Despite knowing that this wasn't going to be a romantic relationship, she was thrilled that she'd bought that sexy dress and shoes. Isaac hadn't seen her at her best. Yet. He wasn't going to know what hit him.

Scout jumped up, barking and chasing his tail as he joined her celebration. Savannah laughed as they danced around the room together. Once she and Scout had exhausted themselves, he returned to his bed and she returned to the couch and her glass of wine.

In the quiet that followed, doubts attacked her. What would Darren think? Would he be disappointed that she'd entered this type of relationship with Isaac with no chance of a future?

Theirs had been a true love. They'd been faithful to each other from the day they'd met. Their hearts had joined before their bodies and his death hadn't changed that.

Her heart still belonged to him. And always would.

Even though, as she drifted off to sleep that night, it was Isaac's face she saw in her dreams.

Savannah stood in front of the full-length, previously ignored mirror in her bathroom and checked her appearance. Jillian had called in a favor and had gotten her hairdresser to squeeze Savannah in that morning before her first appointment. She'd had several inches of split ends cut off and a deep conditioning. Her hair looked better than it had in months.

There had been a cancellation at the spa at Jillian's family's resort where she'd lucked into an appointment for a facial and a mani-pedi. Now her skin glowed and her nails were painted in various shades of red.

It had been so long since she'd pampered herself. There was something so relaxing about having someone massage the pain from her feet and shape and polish her nails. And it was wonderful to have her hair professionally styled. Oddly enough, looking better on the outside had improved the way she felt inside. She'd scheduled an appointment with the stylist and another for a mani-pedi in two weeks' time.

The black dress was just as sexy as she remembered. The low-cut bodice fit smoothly over her breasts, hinting at her body, concealing as much as it revealed. The dress fit snugly around her waist before flaring over her hips and swirling around her thighs, ending several inches above her knees. Her strappy, three-inch heels showcased her calves to their best advantage. She'd added silver bracelets and silver drop earrings. After dabbing perfume that she'd purchased just for tonight on her wrists and behind her ears, she sprayed a mist in the air and stepped into it, and then walked to the living room.

Scout was lying on his bed. When she entered, he sat up, and Savannah could swear the dog did a double take.

"What do you think?"

He barked once.

"The dress isn't too sexy, is it?"

Scout rolled his eyes as if that question was unworthy of a reply.

Sufficiently chastised, Savannah continued. "It's just that I'm nervous. And excited."

Scout barked twice and then walked over to her as if offering reassurance. She rubbed his head and he barked out his best advice before returning to his bed and chew toy. Shaking her head at her foolishness, Savannah went to the window to wait for Isaac to arrive.

"You sure look glum for a man who has a date with a beautiful woman," Miles said after letting Isaac into his house and leading him to the front room.

"I second that emotion," Jillian said, taking Mia from Isaac's arms. Miles and Jillian had volunteered to babysit Mia tonight. When Mia looked askance at being so unceremoniously taken away from her father, Jillian lifted her high into the air, something Mia loved. "I thought this was what you wanted."

"I wanted to take the next step in our relationship. This isn't that."

"I'm confused," Jillian said.

"So am I," Miles added. "Aren't you going out to dinner and then dancing?"

Isaac looked around. "Where are the kids?"

"In the family room watching a movie. They'll be okay for a few minutes."

"Good. I don't want them to hear what I'm going to say."

Miles nodded. "It goes without saying that you're in the vault. We won't repeat anything you say, you know that."

"So, what's wrong? Why isn't this what you wanted?" Jillian asked from her place on the sofa. She'd set Mia into a bouncing chair and was now using one foot to rock the chair, much to Mia's delight.

Isaac sat in a chair across from Jillian and Miles joined her on the sofa. "I wanted to see if we could become more than friends. Savannah wants to be friends with benefits." He made those ridiculous air quotes around his words.

"No," Jillian said.

"Really?" Miles said at the same time. Then they looked at each other and burst into laughter.

"I don't see what's so funny. And thank you for finding humor at the expense of my feelings." He would have expected that type of response from Nathan. But not Miles. And certainly not from Jillian. She'd always been so much more sensitive.

"Sit back down," Miles said. "Nobody is laughing at you."

"No? That sounded like laughter to me," Isaac said. Even though he was still offended, he perched on the edge of the chair, waiting.

"You have to admit the situation is a bit ironic. After all, aren't you the one who refers to yourself as Isaac 'Love and Leave 'em Happy' Montgomery?" Jillian asked.

"I'll be happy not to hear myself called that again."

"Whatever. The point is that you've never wanted a relationship. I don't think you've dated a woman for longer than a week. At least, not to my knowledge. Things could have been different while I was living in Kansas."

"They weren't," Isaac admitted. "But none of the women were looking for anything serious either."

"True," Jillian admitted.

"And now you want something serious," Miles said. Was that pity in his voice? The only thing worse than mockery.

"Maybe Savannah does too," Jillian said, "but

she's learned about your reputation and thinks something is better than nothing."

"Yes and no. Yes, she learned of my reputation, and no, she doesn't want anything else. In fact, she said the only reason she was willing to enter a relationship like this with me is because of my reputation."

"Wow. I didn't see that coming," Miles said.

"So what should I do?"

"I say go for it and enjoy yourself," Miles said without missing a beat.

"What?" Jillian turned to look at Miles. Clearly, she didn't like that response. Isaac wasn't that fond of it, either, but he would bet it was for an entirely different reason. "You cannot be serious."

"Why not? She's a grown woman who knows what she wants."

"Isaac doesn't just want a meaningless sexual relationship. Isaac wants—"

"Isaac is right here," Isaac said, cutting in before things got out of hand. "What I don't want is for the two of you to fight because of me. I just want advice. And I appreciate your point of view, Miles."

"No matter how ridiculous it is," Jillian added. She shook her head at Miles and then turned back to Isaac. "Are you sure you want a real relationship with Savannah? One with a future and commitment? Forever and ever, amen?"

Was he? Honestly, he wasn't certain he was ready

to go that far. He knew that what he wanted from Savannah was more than anything he'd ever wanted with another woman. But forever?

He wasn't ready to risk that. Especially with someone who wouldn't commit to giving him one hundred percent. Heck, she'd been clear that she would never be interested in forever. And he had Mia to think about, too. Mia deserved to be fully loved. Savannah's fear of opening her heart and moving on might make her incapable of even thinking about life with a man who had a child.

"Well?" Jillian prodded him.

"I don't know. Maybe."

"If you want to keep open the possibility, don't go to bed with her."

"Do you mean tonight or ever?" His voice squeaked like an adolescent's.

"Definitely not tonight. And I don't mean not ever. But not soon."

"Why not?" Miles asked.

"I was wondering that myself?" Isaac added.

"You've heard of the friend zone."

"I've heard of it, but I've never actually been inside."

Jillian rolled her eyes. "Guys complain about it all the time. Once you've been slotted as a friend, there is no way of getting a woman to see you any other way. You are no longer boyfriend material."

Isaac nodded. That had never happened to him, thank goodness.

"Well, the same applies in this situation. Right now, Savannah is emerging from her grief. Little by little, she's beginning to let life in. If you become her…boy toy, for lack of a better word, she's never going to see you as a potential partner."

"She says she doesn't want to fall in love again. She doesn't want to risk loving and losing again."

"I understand that. After everything that I went through, I didn't think I would ever love again either. And I certainly didn't expect to fall in love with Miles again. Not after he'd been such a jerk to me."

"I am so sorry for how I hurt you," Miles said sincerely.

"I know," Jillian said softly. She smiled at him and then turned back to Isaac. "Look, Isaac, I don't know Savannah well, so take what I say with a grain of salt. But since you asked for my advice, I'm going to give it to you. Don't go to bed with her under these conditions. If you do, you'll regret it."

"Okay. Thanks." He stood, kissed Mia goodbye and headed for Savannah's house.

As he drove, Jillian's words echoed through his mind. He hated to admit it, but she made a lot of sense. He truly believed that Savannah was overcoming her grief. Oh, he didn't think she would forget her husband and son, or even stop loving them. Nor did he want her to. But he thought she was becoming the woman she'd been before. When she was ready to fully embrace life, he wanted her to see him as a potential partner. If that meant not making love to her now, then so be it.

He parked and then walked up the stairs to her cabin. Before he could ring the bell, the door swung open. And there she was. *Wow.* He'd never seen a sexier woman. It took all of his strength to stick to his vow when he wanted nothing more than to sweep her into his arms and carry her to bed. When he realized his mouth had dropped open, he snapped it shut and stepped inside.

"Wow. You are positively stunning."

Savannah turned in a slow circle, her hips swaying seductively. "This old thing?"

Isaac smiled. Suddenly, his tie felt tight and he ran a finger around his shirt collar. "That old thing."

"Thanks. And might I say that you look pretty good yourself."

Isaac struck a pose. "This old thing? I just reached into my closet and pulled out the first thing I touched."

She tapped his chest and the blood began pulsing in his veins. "You chose well."

Isaac was momentarily struck speechless. What was wrong with him? This wasn't his first date by a long shot. *Get a grip.* He needed to pull it together

before she changed her mind and ran away from
him again. "Are you ready to go?"

"Just let me grab my wrap."

She picked up her purse and a long piece of silk.
He held out his hand. "Let me help you with that."

Savannah placed the fabric into his hands and
then turned her back to him. She lifted her gorgeous hair and her sweet scent wafted toward his
nose. He didn't know the name of the perfume she
was wearing, but he knew that he liked it.

When he only stood there, Savannah glanced
over her shoulder at him. The curious look on her
face shook him out of his stupor and he draped the
fabric across her shoulders. He let his hand linger
for a moment as he caressed her skin. Sexual tension
arced between them, and Isaac reminded himself
that he was playing the long game. He wanted to
keep open the possibility of having a real relationship with her. So no matter how much he desired
her, when the night ended, he was going to kiss her
goodbye and head on home.

No matter if it killed him.

"Tell me more about what it was like to grow
up in Aspen Creek," Savannah said as they drove
down the highway. She'd been surprised when she'd
stepped onto her porch beside Isaac and seen the
luxury sedan in her driveway. It definitely was a
step up from his SUV.

"What do you want to know?"

Savannah turned in her comfortable leather seat so that she could get a better look at him. She'd been serious when she'd told him that he looked good. Dressed in a navy suit, crisp white shirt that looked stunning against his brown skin, and a blue tie, he looked like a male model. He'd pulled his locks into a ponytail, revealing his high cheekbones. His beard and mustache were neatly trimmed.

When he'd stepped close to her, she'd caught a whiff of his cologne. He smelled so good that her knees had actually weakened. She tried to tell herself that her attraction was strictly physical, but she knew that was only partially true. Sure, Isaac was sexy as hell. His muscles were well formed and a clear sign that he did a lot of physical work each day. Although he had a great body, that was only part of his appeal. He was smart, considerate, funny and an all-around good man. She really liked and admired him. But since those feelings didn't align with her friends-with-benefits plan, she decided to ignore them.

"Whatever you want to tell me."

"I told you a little about life on the ranch. The fun we had as kids and teens."

"I remember. And it sounds great."

"Aspen Creek is home to a lot of winter Olympians. A couple of them have schools where they teach skiing or skating, though most of them are happy teaching classes at the resorts. I learned how to ski from a gold medalist."

"Really? That's impressive."

"I didn't understand how big a deal it was back then. After all, he was just one of the people you pass on the street. You know?"

She nodded, and he continued. "Although Aspen Creek is a world-famous resort town now, it wasn't always. It was just another small town in Colorado. Until about twenty-five years ago, only the locals knew about us. Now we get everyone from rich Europeans coming for a couple of weeks in the snow, to people from Denver coming to spend a day on the slopes.

"Downtown used to consist of two stores that carried everything, the diner and one semi-fancy restaurant. Now it has everything you can imagine. Exclusive boutiques, jewelry stores, five-star restaurants, clubs and a theater. We have our fair share of tourist traps, but luckily there are also places that only the townspeople know about. And despite the changes, we have managed to remain a close-knit community."

"Are we going to a tourist restaurant or a place where the locals go?"

"Both. The food is delicious and the restaurant is well-known throughout the state."

"I'm looking forward to it." She paused for a moment. "So what do you do when you're not working? Are there any clubs you like more than others?"

"Well, as a rancher, I need to get up early, but that didn't stop me from hanging out a few weekdays and every weekend. My older brother, Nathan, likes to lecture me like I'm a kid, but he's all work and no play. He actually has a ten-page five-year plan. But that was all before Mia. Now I'm all about fatherhood. I haven't been to a club since I became a father."

She circled back to something he said. "How old are you?"

"I'm twenty-five."

"Wow. That's all! I thought you were a lot older than that."

He grinned. "I'm of legal age. I can consent to whatever we do."

"I know that." She chuckled. "I'm older than you are."

"So what?"

"I'm thirty-three. That's eight years."

"Is that going to be a problem for you?"

She thought about it. It wasn't as if they were going to have a real relationship. They were just having fun, so the age difference didn't matter. And as he'd pointed out, he was an adult. "No."

"Good."

"Tell me more about these clubs."

"There are three that I used to go to regularly.

Two only the townspeople and ranchers know about. They aren't ritzy, but they have good drinks and good, if limited, menus. All three of them have great DJs."

"Which one are we going to?"

"I thought we'd hit Grady's. It's a club the locals like. They have a great house band in addition to a popular DJ."

Savannah nodded as an unfamiliar feeling of excitement began to grow within her. It had been so long since she'd danced or gone to a club. Her heart began beating faster and she knew that she was in for a good time.

When they arrived at the restaurant, Isaac parked. Savannah made a move to open her door and Isaac placed his hand on her wrist. She looked at him quizzically.

"I'll get that for you."

Savannah controlled her breathing as she watched Isaac cross in front of the car and toward her door. His stride was the confident walk of a man who knew where he was going and how he intended to get there. And for the time being, she would be by his side, accompanying him.

He opened her door and then helped her from her seat. It was a small thing that might not have made a difference on any other night, but her senses were on high alert.

He took her hand as they walked to the front of

the restaurant and stepped inside. A young woman stood at a podium. When she saw them, she smiled. "Good evening. Party of two?"

"Yes. The reservation is under the name Montgomery."

She glanced at a paper then grabbed two menus. "Follow me. Your table is ready."

Savannah and Isaac followed the hostess through the restaurant to a spot near a window. As Savannah walked, she glanced around, impressed by the ambience. Crystal chandeliers hung from the ceiling and, coupled with the flickering candles on the tables, created a romantic atmosphere. Her feet sank into the plush carpet as she wove through the maze of tables covered with white cloths.

When they reached their table, Isaac held out her chair, helping her to sit before taking his seat across from her. Delicious aromas floated on the air and her mouth began to water.

As they perused their menus, Savannah lowered hers slightly and peered at Isaac over the top. He looked so delicious, a part of her wanted to skip dinner and dancing and head back to her place. But part of the thrill of the night was the anticipation. If she could ever love again, she might take things differently and really get to know Isaac. But since her heart still belonged to her husband, there was no chance of a future with Isaac.

"What's good?" she asked, pulling her thoughts

back to the here and now before the negative ones could ruin the moment.

"You'll be safe choosing anything. Of course, the beef comes from our ranch, so you might want to stick with a steak. If by some odd chance you don't like beef, all of the chicken and fish options are delicious."

"I like a good steak, so that's what I'll have."

When their waiter came, they placed their orders and then leaned back in their chairs. Savannah had never lacked for topics of conversation, but now words failed her. Fortunately for her, Isaac had no such difficulty and he regaled her with humorous tales of ranch life that kept her laughing from scrumptious appetizers to the last bite of their delicious main courses.

"Do you have room for dessert?" he asked.

"Only if they have tiny ones."

"We could share."

She nodded at the notion. They decided on white chocolate mousse. When it arrived, Isaac picked up the spoon, scooped up some, and held the spoon up to her lips. Her heart raced as she opened her mouth. The chilled dessert was delicious, and she moaned with pleasure.

"Good?"

"You have no idea."

Using the same utensil, he spooned some mousse

into his mouth. A smile tugged at his sexy lips. "Perfect."

She picked up her own spoon and began to eat. They didn't talk as they shared the dessert, but the air zinged with sexual tension, matching the desire building within her.

Once they'd scraped the last bit of sweetness from the dish, he smiled at her. "Ready to go?"

"Yes."

He paid the bill and left a nice tip for the server before escorting Savannah from the restaurant. The sun had been setting when they'd arrived and now night had settled in earnest. A cool breeze blew and she moved closer to Isaac.

"Cold?" He took off his suit jacket, draped it over her shoulders and pulled her closer to his side.

The jacket was warm from his body heat and retained a hint of his enticing cologne. Nothing could feel better. "Not anymore." Now she was hot.

"The club is a few blocks away, so perhaps we should drive."

"We don't have to do that. After that incredible meal, I could use a walk. Besides, I've walked these streets many a night."

"I know. I've seen you a couple of times when I was leaving a club or restaurant. What's up with that?"

"Insomnia." A half-truth. "Exercise helps."

"You come a long way for that."

She decided to trust him with the rest of the truth. "Loneliness. I live on a beautiful piece of land, but it's isolated. Or, at least, I thought it was. I didn't realize how close you were."

"I'm there. But on the nights that I saw you, you were always alone. Were you meeting someone?"

"No. I didn't want to talk to anyone, but I was tired of my own thoughts. It was enough to know that people were nearby. Every once in a while, I stopped in the all-night diner for a meal."

"You didn't have to be alone. You could have struck up a conversation with anyone."

"I know. But I wasn't ready. I needed time to decide if and how I wanted to rejoin society."

"And then I barged into your life and dragged you back into the world."

She laughed. "That's not how I would describe it. Being around you and your family has been good. You are all so warm and welcoming. It reminded me of what I was missing."

"You don't have to miss out on anything, Savannah. Not as long as I'm around."

He sounded so sincere and Savannah knew what he was offering. A real relationship. A future with him and Mia. The idea wasn't scary enough to send her running into the night, but it wasn't exactly comforting either.

And it wasn't what she wanted.

Chapter Eleven

Isaac felt Savannah withdraw from him and he wanted to kick himself. He'd come on too strong. Savannah had been clear that she wasn't interested in anything other than a friendly sexual relationship. Real emotions—and real conversations—were off-limits. Although that wasn't what he wanted, it's what he'd agreed to. Sure he hoped for more, but he wouldn't get more by behaving like the battering ram Savannah had once called him. He had to give her a chance to grow comfortable with the idea that they could have a richer, deeper relationship than that. It had to be a decision she reached on her own.

Making statements that promised a future was certain to guarantee they didn't have one.

Saying nothing was the best way not to say the

wrong thing, so he kept his mouth shut as they walked down the street. Once he was certain the uncomfortable moment was behind them, he changed the subject to the band they were going to hear tonight. "The house band—Downhill From Here—is really good. The drummer and bass player actually work as studio musicians, and they've played on some hit albums."

"So you're telling me I'm about to meet some celebrities?" Savannah asked.

"I wouldn't call Rodney and Garrett celebrities," Isaac said, smiling at her. She seemed so excited at the prospect that he hated to burst her bubble. "They play for some pretty big names now and again. Rodney actually went on a six-month world tour a few years ago, but he hated all the travel. Said he got sick of hotels and never knowing what city he was in."

"I don't know. That sounds pretty exciting to me. Glamorous, you know? Paris. London. Rome. Sign me up."

"Cleveland. Indianapolis. Boise."

She laughed. "Admittedly less glamorous, but places I wouldn't mind visiting if it meant I could be in a band."

"Rodney is a friendly guy. So's Garrett, for that matter. If we have a chance, I'll introduce you to them. You might even take the opportunity to sing a few bars for them. Who knows, you might discover a new career. Do you have any hidden talent?"

"Yeah, it's even hidden from me. You're the one who should be auditioning."

"Nah. I have no interest in a singing career."

"That's too bad because you have a great voice."

"I'll let you in on a little secret."

"What?"

They'd reached the club and stepped inside. It was early enough for them to grab a table near the stage. They flagged down a waitress and ordered drinks. Once the place began to fill up, it would be hard to hold a conversation, but that wasn't a problem now. After their beverages arrived, Savannah took a sip and then turned back to Isaac.

"Now, what's that secret?"

"Well, I shouldn't have called it a secret because a lot of people know. When we were kids, my brothers and I had a band. We sang and some of our friends played instruments. We entered a couple of talent contests."

"Really?" Her beautiful smile lit up her face. "How did you do?"

"We came in third for one and second in the other."

"What happened?"

"It took a lot of time. Practicing wasn't as much fun as riding horses, skiing or playing hockey. After one loud knock-down, drag-out fight, we broke up. Our illustrious career—" he grinned so she would know he was joking "—ended as quickly as it started."

"Even so, I'll count you among the nearly famous."

"Like those people on reality shows? No thanks."

She laughed and wrinkled her nose. She looked so cute, Isaac couldn't help but laugh with her. Although he could hear her perfectly well, he leaned closer. "Now tell me, do you have any talents I need to know about?"

"I can't carry a tune in a basket."

"What about juggling? Or magic?"

"Sorry, no."

"How about spinning plates on sticks? Tumbling?"

"Do you think I ran away from the circus? Are you trying to call me a clown?"

"Not at all. You are the furthest thing from a clown that I've ever seen."

"That was the right answer. Of course, all of this talk about the circus has me wanting cotton candy. Or popcorn."

"Sorry, this isn't that kind of club. But if you play your cards right, I'll take you to the movies tomorrow and though I can't promise cotton candy, you can get popcorn."

"So we're going out tomorrow too?"

"If you're free."

She gave him a long look and he would have given anything to know what that look meant. Finally, she nodded. "I'm free. What's showing?"

"I have no idea. But before you get your hopes up, let me warn you that the theater only has two screens and I bet neither of the movies is a new release. So if you have something particular in mind, we might need to go to Denver."

"I have no idea what movies are out. Besides, I kind of like the idea of going to a small-town theater and watching whatever they show. It's charming."

"I'm glad you think that. As a teenager, it was limiting. Not that we spent all that much time inside. Living here, there were plenty of things to do outside all year round. That said, it was a lot easier to neck with a girl in the back of a movie theater than on a snowy mountaintop."

"I imagine you were just as popular with the girls then as you are now."

"I could say it was a new thing, but that wouldn't be the truth. And I'll always tell you the truth. Women have always seemed to like me." He shrugged. "It's one of life's great mysteries."

Savannah's eyes traveled over his torso and then his face. "If you looked anything like you do now, the mystery is solved."

Isaac felt his cheeks grow hot and he grabbed his cola and took a long drink, searching for an appropriate response. What kind of man blushed because a woman complimented him? He wasn't vain, but he wasn't one for false modesty either. He knew that women found him attractive.

The band took the stage right then, saving him from a need to reply.

The drummer pounded out the beat and then the

guitars and horns joined in. By the time the lead singer began to sing, all conversation had ceased, and everyone turned their attention to the stage. Isaac glanced over at Savannah. She was snapping her fingers and swaying to the music. When she caught him staring at her, she smiled brightly and continued chair-dancing. It was good to see her enjoying herself. After all that she'd lost in the past, she deserved to let herself go and have fun. He wondered if she held herself back out of a misguided sense of loyalty to her deceased husband and child. Or guilt.

"What's wrong?" Savannah asked.

"Nothing. I'm just glad to see that you like the band."

"They're good. But I'm sure they're not better than the Montgomery Three or whatever you called yourself." She flashed a mischievous grin.

"I should never have told you about that," he said with a laugh.

"Oh yes, you most definitely should have."

They turned their attention back to the band who had ended the first song and segued into the next. After the first set ended, the crowd roared and jumped to their feet.

"They're really good," Savannah said, applauding.

"So's the DJ. Ready to dance?"

They were already standing, so when the first song started, all they had to do was step onto the dance floor. After seeing Savannah's first few moves, Isaac was impressed. She did know how to dance, which was good. There was nothing worse than being partnered with someone who couldn't keep up with him.

The first three songs were up-tempo, and Isaac got pleasure watching Savannah shimmy her sexy body. Her moves were enticing and seductive, holding a promise of even more pleasure to come. Too bad he wouldn't be indulging in any other kind of pleasure with Savannah tonight.

When the DJ played a ballad, Isaac held out his arms and Savannah instantly stepped into them. He wrapped his arms around her waist and pulled her close. She fit so perfectly against him. She leaned her head on his chest and he heard her soft sigh as she snuggled closer. Her sweet scent surrounded him and he breathed deeply, taking her in. *I could get used to this.*

Savannah lifted her head and he saw the desire burning in her eyes. Despite the promise he'd made to himself earlier, he couldn't ignore the invitation. Leaning down, he brushed his lips against hers. Heat shot through his body and desire flamed to life. She opened her mouth to him, welcoming him inside, and his tongue tangled with hers. Savannah wrapped her arms around his neck, pulling him closer to her. He gave in to his desire, cupping her soft bottom and pressing her against him.

She moaned and awareness of their surroundings intruded on the moment, dousing the flame. They were in the middle of a club, surrounded by dozens of people.

Although he had a reputation, he had always behaved with the decorum his parents had instilled in him. He pulled back, noting with satisfaction that Savannah held on to him for several moments before releasing him. He gradually regained control of his labored breathing and his pulse slowed. The song was still playing, so they resumed dancing without missing a beat.

They danced two more slow songs, their bodies pressed snugly together, before the DJ announced that the band would be returning to play their second set. Isaac reluctantly released Savannah and they held hands as they returned to their table. Isaac usually enjoyed the Downhill From Here, but he was distracted by Savannah's nearness and spent as much time watching her as he did the band.

The band ended their set with a flourish and then invited everyone to stay and party with the DJ.

"Do you want to dance some more?" Isaac asked, not sure of the answer he wanted.

"Would you think I was a party pooper if I said no?"

"Not at all. We can sit here and listen to the music if you want."

"Actually, what I want is to move the party

home." She placed her hand on his and slipped her fingers between his. He flipped over his hand, pressing their palms together.

He hesitated as he thought back to the promise he'd made to himself. He intended to keep it, but making out wasn't be breaking that vow. "I can get with that." *WOULDN'T*

"Then let's go."

Isaac kept his arm around her waist, holding her close to his side as they walked through the club. They stepped outside, and the chilly wind that greeted them did little to cool his desires. As they began walking back to the car, he noticed that Savannah was taking mincing steps. Isaac looked at her feet. "Those shoes must be killing your feet. I should have thought of that before and driven here from the restaurant."

"No worries. I'll just take them off."

"You're going to walk barefoot? On the sidewalk?"

"Don't sound so appalled. Women do it all the time." She bent over, released the straps on her shoes and then slid out one foot and then the other. Grabbing her shoes and letting them dangle from her fingers, she took a step. She sighed. "That's so much better."

"Hold on," Isaac said. It didn't sit right with him. He untied his shoes and took them off.

She stared at him. "What are you doing?"

"If you're going barefoot, I am too."

"You really don't have to do that."

"Sure I do," he said. He removed his socks and shoved them into his shoes. The ground was cold beneath his feet. Luckily, it was dry. She didn't say anything else, but she smiled.

He held out a hand and she took it. As they walked together down the street, he felt her eyes on him. "What are you looking at, Savannah?"

"Nothing. I just didn't expect you to be so…"

"So what?"

"I don't know." Her full lips twisted as she searched for a word. She looked positively sexy. "I've just never known a man to walk down the street without his shoes before because the woman with him did."

"Maybe their feet aren't as attractive as mine."

She laughed and tugged at his arm. "I'm being serious. It's thoughtful. And I appreciate it."

He nodded, although since it was dark, he wasn't sure that she saw it.

They walked through the quiet streets without speaking. The trees rustled in the breeze and an owl hooted in the distance. Once they reached the car, he held open her door for her. When she was inside, she slipped on her heels again and leaned back against the seat. It took him a little longer to put on his shoes and socks, but once he was done, he vowed to park closer to the destination the next time they went out.

Savannah hummed one of the songs the band had played as they pulled away from the curb. When they hit the highway, she turned on the radio and they both sang along to the popular song.

"Were you the lead singer?" she asked.

"No, Nathan was. He's the oldest, so he said he should be the lead singer even though Miles has the best voice by far."

"Ruining your chance for the big time and keeping the Montgomery Brothers from getting out of this hick town."

"Is that what you think of Aspen Creek? That we're a hick town?" He knew it wasn't a bustling metropolis with all of the attractions that big cities had, but to him Aspen Creek was the best place in the world to live. He wanted to raise Mia and any other children he was blessed to have here. He'd hoped that Savannah would see the charm and want to make a home here. But perhaps she didn't. Aspen Creek had been a refuge for her. Maybe once she was healed and ready to rejoin society, she would kick the dust of this town from her feet and find a place that suited her better.

"Not at all. I like it here. But it fits the story of the Montgomery Family Singers better, don't you think?"

"I think you're never going to let it die."

"You got that right," she said with a wicked grin. "This is too good a story to let go by the wayside."

Isaac didn't mind the teasing one bit. He liked how happy joking about the band made Savannah. As long as she got a kick out of it, he'd let her make fun of the short-lived band. He'd do anything to make her happy.

Anything to prove to her that if she tried opening her heart again, he'd make damn sure she never regretted it.

Savannah enjoyed the ride to the cabin immensely. Teasing Isaac was so much fun. He was so good-natured. Unflappable. Nothing seemed to bother him. But he wasn't a pushover. He gave as good as he got even though she suspected that he was being extra careful of her feelings. She wanted to tell him that she wouldn't break if he made fun of her, but she wasn't entirely sure that was true. She wasn't quite sure where the cracks in her facade lay. The reason she was in Aspen Creek was in part due to her inability to cope with the hand life had dealt her.

He turned into her driveway just in time to keep her from pursuing those depressing thoughts. The moment she had been looking forward to all night had finally arrived. She didn't want anything bringing her down tonight.

Just as he had earlier in the evening, he came

around the car to open the door for her. As the night progressed, she'd grown accustomed to his chivalrous ways. In addition to opening her car door, he'd stood when she'd left the table and stayed on the outside as they'd strolled down the street.

Now he took her hand as they walked together to her front door. Her heart began to pound in anticipation. A night of no-strings sex was just what she needed. She would feel alive again if only for a few hours. A few hours of bliss that would sweep away the pain.

Her hand trembled as she tried to unlock the door and she realized she was nervous. Though she was trying to be blasé, this was a big deal. Isaac steadied her hand and together they inserted the key, turned it, and then twisted the doorknob. He opened her door and stood aside, letting her go before him. She'd left a lamp on, and it cast a romantic glow. She tossed her purse and wrap on a chair and then turned to glance at him.

He was standing stiffly in the doorway. That didn't bode well for the night of mindless pleasure she'd envisioned. Maybe he wasn't sure she was still willing. "Would you like a drink?"

Truth be told, she could use something to steady her nerves.

His chest rose and fell as he inhaled. He didn't reply for several long seconds and dread filled her.

"No, thank you. It's getting late and I need to get going."

"What? I thought that we had plans for the night."

"I know what you thought. And as appealing as staying the night sounds, I'm going to have to decline."

She dropped onto the sofa. What was even happening? She knew Isaac was attracted to her. They'd danced close together all night and certain things couldn't be faked. Or hidden. "I don't understand. I thought you agreed to be friends with benefits. What changed?"

"Nothing."

"Then... What's going on? Did you change your mind?"

"No, I didn't." He sat beside her, took her hand and looked into her eyes. "I don't see how we can be friends with benefits without being friends. *Real* friends."

"You don't think we're friends?"

"I think we are becoming friends. But I would like to be close friends before anything becomes physical."

"Being physical will bring us closer."

"Not in the way that I mean. The kind of friendship I want develops over time. Friendship that comes from being a part of each other's lives. Then we can move on and be friends with benefits."

"I don't think that's necessary for friends with

benefits." She leaned closer and kissed his neck. He closed his eyes briefly. She heard the hitch in his breath and smiled. She reached up to loosen his tie.

He caught her hand and pulled away. "It's necessary for me. Anything short of that and I'll feel used. Like I'm nothing but a booty call."

He might be overstating things, but she got the message. The depth of disappointment was a surprise. It wasn't as if she was in love with Isaac. She barely knew him.

That thought brought her up short. That was exactly Isaac's point. He wanted to be actual friends. The idea was a bit frightening. She already liked and admired him, and they seemed to have a lot in common, so becoming close friends would be easy. But what then?

Admittedly, he made her life better. He'd managed to chase away the loneliness that had constantly tracked her. The shroud of grief that had wrapped around her in the months since Darren and Tony's deaths had begun to loosen. Isaac had played a big part in that. And she didn't want to go back to life without him. So, despite being sexually frustrated and the fact that this wasn't the way that she wanted tonight to go, she would accept his decision.

"So what do we do now?"

He exhaled and she realized that he had been worried about her reaction. "Now we go to the movies. And if you like to hike, we can do that. If you want, we can go horseback riding again. Do you fish? Like water sports? Can you swim? There are so many things we can do together. All you have to do is say yes."

"And you'll do the rest?"

"No. You'll be an equal partner and *together* we'll find fun ways to spend time while getting to know each other."

Just not in bed. "That sounds good."

"On that note, I should get going. I need to pick up Mia and get her home."

He stood and she walked beside him to the door. When they were there, he turned, swept her into his arms and gave her a kiss so hot she practically melted at his feet. Then he opened the door and left her standing there, on fire. Even the cold wind didn't cool her off.

She might have agreed to put the benefits on hold, but after that kiss, she knew it wasn't going to be easy.

Chapter Twelve

Although Savannah understood Isaac's perspective, that hadn't made falling asleep any easier. She'd tossed and turned for hours before finally drifting into a fitful sleep. In her dreams, she'd continued to reach out for him. Whenever she got close enough to kiss him, he would laugh and move just out of reach. It was aggravating, and when she awoke, she was just as frustrated as she'd been last night.

She was groggy and preferred to stay in bed, but Scout demanded to be let out. Savannah hoped the fresh morning air would clear her head; it helped very little. As she tossed the ball in a never-ending game of fetch, she tried to think straight, but it was impossible. There were too many conflicting emotions battling for dominance inside her for her mind to be anything other than a jumbled mess.

When her arm began to cramp up, she tossed the ball one last time then went inside to make breakfast. Instead of eating, she found herself using her bacon to draw circles in her grits. In the past when she'd had a hard decision to make, she'd turned to her best friend, Cheris, who'd always helped her find clarity. Cheris had always known the right questions to ask. Probing questions to help Savannah distill the problem to its essence, order her priorities, and then find a way forward.

Savannah hadn't talked to Cheris since they'd fallen out in the weeks following Darren and Tony's deaths. Savannah knew that she owed her friend an apology, yet she hadn't reached out. What was she waiting for? Cheris had been there for Savannah during difficult times and Savannah had done the same for her. She sighed. Now was the time to make that call and seek forgiveness. Cheris deserved that. And if they were able to rekindle their relationship...well, all the better.

Grabbing her phone, she dialed Cheris's number and listened while the phone rang.

"Hello?" Cheris's cheery voice sounded so familiar that Savannah's throat clogged and, for a minute, she couldn't speak. Tears flooded her eyes.

"Hello?" Cheris repeated. Savannah could hear the smile in her voice.

"Hi." Savannah brushed tears from her face. She didn't know why she was crying, but she couldn't seem to stop. Her voice had come out rough and ragged, so she cleared her throat and tried again. "Hi. It's me. Savannah."

"Savannah?" Cheris shrieked.

"Yes. Is now a good time to talk?"

"Are you kidding me? I've been wanting to hear from you for forever. I've been hoping you would call. Or email. Send a card. Anything to let me know that you were okay. Yes, it's a good time."

Savannah launched into her apology. "I'm so sorry for how I acted. You approached me from a place of love, and I cut you out of my life. That was wrong. Can you forgive me?"

"I owe you an apology too. For not understanding how devastated you were. I felt helpless seeing you in so much pain. I didn't know how to help you. I should have realized that I didn't have to help you heal. You just needed me to be there, letting you heal in your own time. I'm sorry I didn't know how to do that."

Though it wasn't a long speech and Cheris's words came out in a hurried jumble, they were exactly what Savannah needed to hear. The part of her heart that had been smashed by her best friend's actions began knitting itself back together. They'd each made mistakes—Savannah could see that now—but the mistakes weren't insurmountable.

"Let's just agree to put the past behind us and move on from here."

"Agreed." There was a pause before Cheris continued. "So, where are you? Where did you go? I stopped by your house a year ago and there was a For Sale sign on it. I checked at the university and was told you weren't teaching any classes."

"A resort town in Colorado. Aspen Creek."

"What made you go there? Do you know someone there?"

Savannah explained about getting in her car and driving away from Madison in a futile attempt to outrun the pain. "Basically, it was as good a place as any. I've been living in a cabin on a ranch. A little isolated, but it was what I needed. Hiding, if you want to know the truth. For a long time, I kept to myself because I didn't want to make any attachments. Recently, I've begun to meet people. Well, a couple of people. My neighbors."

"Does that mean you won't be moving back to Madison?"

Emotion filled her throat. "There's nothing left for me there. Only painful memories. Honestly, the thought of coming back makes me sick to my stomach. My house sold not too long after I listed it. I should probably let my dean know that my sabbatical is going to turn into a resignation."

"Although I feel the need to point out that I'm here, as well as the rest of your friends who have all been concerned about you, I completely understand. From where I'm sitting, a fresh start in a new place looks pretty good. I've been thinking about getting one myself."

"Really? I don't think Gerald will go for that. His roots in Madison run deep. As do yours."

"Gerald and I broke up over six months ago, so I no longer consider his opinion when making my decisions."

Savannah realized that time might have stood still for her, but it hadn't for everyone else. The world had continued to turn. "Oh no. What happened? I thought for sure you were going to get married."

"So did I. I was wrong. He was cheating on me. And that is all I care to say about him."

Savannah heard the pain in her friend's voice and searched for something comforting to say. Nothing came to mind. "The subject is closed unless and until you open it."

"Thank you."

"One day you'll find someone worthy of you." The minute the platitude rolled off her tongue, Savannah wanted to call it back. What had made her say something so inane? The words had come out before she'd had a chance to give them any thought. Because her friend was in pain, and she'd wanted to make it all better.

Just as her friends had done when Darren and Tony died.

"Maybe. But I certainly am not going to waste time looking for him. Enough about me. I want to know about you. That is, if there's something you want to talk about."

Savannah heard the anxiety in her friend's voice and realized their relationship was still a bit shaky. But then, since they hadn't talked in a very long time, that should be expected. Savannah believed that it would rebound given time and attention. "Actually, there is. I just don't know where to start."

"Beginning. Middle. End. Anywhere works for me. Just start talking and I'll follow along."

Savannah sucked in a breath and then jumped right in. "I recently became friends with a man. He's a really good guy and I..." She had always told Cheris everything, but suddenly she found herself unable to spit out the words. After the way she'd told everyone that there would never be anyone in her life who could compare to Darren, how would Cheris respond when she told her about Isaac? And what she'd proposed.

"What? Are you getting remarried?"

"Of course not. I'm not in love with him." Her voice lacked the conviction it should have held, giving Savannah momentary pause.

"Then what? Whatever it is, I'm sure it's all right."

"I suggested that we be friends with benefits."

"Okay."

"That's it? That's all you're going to say?"

"Well, yeah. I'm certainly not going to criticize you, if that's what you were expecting."

"Especially since I already cut you out of my life once for saying your piece."

"Well, there's that. But that's not what I was going to say."

"Then what?"

"You're thirty-three years old, so sexual desires are natural."

"So you don't think this...cheapens the act?"

"Girl, please. We're talking about having sex, not scribbling a mustache on the *Mona Lisa*."

Savannah couldn't help but laugh. "I guess."

"I *know.* So what did he say?"

"Yes. Sort of. Last night we went to dinner and dancing. I was primed and ready when he brought me home, envisioning a night of hot, sweaty sex. He stayed for a few minutes and left. According to him, friends with benefits means we have to be *friends* first."

Cheris laughed. "Really? That's a first for me. I don't think I've met a man who turned down the benefits on the grounds that the friendship hadn't been established yet. He sounds like a keeper."

"But I don't want to keep him."

"Why not?"

"Because he's not Darren."

There was a long pause. When Cheris spoke again, her voice was gentle. "Nobody will ever be Darren. But Darren is gone. As much as we both wish otherwise, he won't be coming back."

Even though she knew that, hearing the words still hurt. Made her eyes well with unshed tears. "I know. And I like Isaac. He's totally different from Darren, but being around him feels right."

"Then why are you trying to keep from having a real relationship with him?"

"I told him that I didn't want to hurt him, and that's true. I don't know if I'm able to love him or anybody else. But I'm also scared to open myself up. I can't let myself be devastated again."

"I know what you mean. He might turn out to be a jerk."

"I'm not worried about that," Savannah replied quickly. "He's a good man. A great man even. But I'm afraid of loving him and losing him the way I lost Darren and Tony."

"What happened to them was a tragedy. I wish I could promise you that nothing like that would ever happen again, but I can't. But by trying to avoid pain, you could be throwing away a chance to be happy again."

"He has a daughter. Mia's almost a year old."

"Oh."

"She's so adorable. She has such a sunny personality. I could love her but, Cheris, I…can't."

"You're scared."

"Terrified."

"Does saying the word out loud change your feelings?"

"Not one bit." Savannah blew out a breath. "What should I do?"

"Become his friend and then get all of the benefits that you can."

Savannah couldn't hold back her laughter. Cheris always managed to lift her spirits. "You're serious, aren't you?"

"Yep. You've been honest about what you want and what you can and cannot give, and you both agreed to the terms. So have fun and get all of the mind-blowing sex that you can."

"If you say so."

"I do. And speaking of mind-blowing sex, does this Isaac have a brother?"

"Two. Although I've only met one, and he's engaged."

"That's okay. I'll take the other one, sight unseen."

Savannah laughed. It felt good to talk with her friend again. "You know, if you want to get away for a while, I have room here. I think you'd like Aspen Creek."

"It's tempting."

"Think about it."

They talked for a while longer and Cheris caught

Savannah up on the goings-on of her former co-workers and friends. By the time they ended their call with a promise to talk again in a few days, Savannah was feeling optimistic about her relationship with Isaac. She was confident she could be his friend while keeping her heart protected.

She just hoped Isaac would be able to do the same.

"Stop screaming," Isaac said with a chuckle. "You're scaring all of the birds out of the trees."

As if proving his point, a dozen birds took to flight in the clear blue sky.

They were at his favorite secluded fishing hole on the ranch, enjoying the unseasonably warm and sunny day. At least he was enjoying it. The jury was still out on Savannah.

"Then take this pole and get this thing away from me," Savannah said. "This isn't as much fun as I thought it would be."

"That's because you're panicking over nothing. I never thought that you would be afraid of a little fish."

"I don't want that thing touching me."

"It's nowhere near you. It's still in the water." He shook his head. "I guess you aren't the outdoors type."

"Are you kidding me? I went hiking and swimming and even sailing. And I had a great time. But fishing is a whole other…"

"Kettle of fish?" Isaac supplied.

She rolled her eyes. "Yes. So take this pole and you finish catching it. I'll watch and admire your form."

"No can do." Isaac leaned his fishing rod against his camp chair and walked over to Savannah.

"I'll drop this thing," she threatened. The pole jerked in her hand and she shrieked again.

"Let me help you." He stood behind her and then wrapped his arm around her waist. Pulling her closer to him, he put his hands over hers. The pole shook as the fish yanked against the line, struggling to get away.

Savannah whimpered. Although he couldn't see her face, he would bet that her eyes were squeezed shut.

"Don't fight, Savannah," Isaac said. "You just hold on and let the fish tire itself out. See, it's getting tired already. It won't be long now. Now all you have to do is reel it in."

Isaac placed Savannah's hand on the wheel and together they spun it until the fish was dangling on the line a few inches in front of their faces.

"Oh," Savannah said. Her voice was a mixture of horror and shock.

"This is a good size. Definitely big enough for lunch."

"Lunch? Surely you don't intend for us to eat him."

"Him? Yes. I actually do intend for us to eat *it*.

I know you eat fish. We had some the other day at the diner."

"That was totally different. That was strange fish. I didn't know it. But I've bonded with this fish, so there's no way he's going to be my lunch."

"You *bonded* with this fish? When? How is that even possible?"

"Just now. We've both just shared a traumatic experience and there is no way I'm eating Nemo now. So just let him go back to his family."

Isaac swallowed a retort and shook his head. He wasn't going to win this argument. Not when she'd named the fish after a hero in an animated movie. He removed the hook from the fish's mouth and then dropped it back into the lake.

"Be free, Nemo. And stay away from hooks," Savannah called as the fish swam off.

"You know Nemo was a clown fish. That was a walleye."

"What? So you think there's only one fish in the world named Nemo?"

"Fish in the wild don't have names."

She ignored him. "And *this* Nemo and I are friends. And I don't eat my friends."

"You do realize that I'm a cattle rancher, right?"

Savannah rolled her eyes for the second time in fifteen minutes. She looked just as cute this time as the first. "Of course I know that. I live next door to you."

"Cattle ranches are known for their beef. Ours is some of the best in the country."

"I know. I've tasted it. But if there's a point, you might want to get around to making it."

"We don't name our cows. They aren't our *pets*. Or our *friends*."

"Good for you. But *that* has nothing to do with *this*. Nemo was my friend and I wasn't going to eat him."

"But you'll eat fish and steak."

"I fail to see your point. Do you even have a point?"

"Are you going to bond with every fish we catch?"

"I'm not going to catch any more fish and traumatize them, so your question is moot."

"Okay. Well, then, I guess our fishing trip is over."

Savannah placed her hand on his forearm, holding him in place. She looked equal parts remorseful and determined. She wouldn't be changing her mind. Nor did he want her to. "I hope I didn't ruin things."

"Not at all." He covered her hand with his. "I just want to be with you. I don't care what we do or don't do."

She leaned her forehead against his shoulder and he felt the tension leaving her body. "I feel the same way."

"Then let's get back to the house."

They packed up their gear and mounted their horses. Over the past two weeks, Isaac and Savannah had spent a lot of time together. He couldn't recall laughing this much with a woman or having this much fun. The more time he spent with her, the more time he wanted to spend with her. Isaac felt closer to Savannah than he had to any other woman. Even though they'd taken in the sights in Aspen Creek, he'd enjoyed the quiet times just as much. It was as much fun sitting on his deck and staring up at the stars as it was going to Denver to see a traveling Broadway show.

There was only one thing that kept their relationship from being perfect. Savannah was holding herself back from Mia. Oh, she was kind to her. She played with her and read to her. But she was emotionally distant. At her age, Mia probably couldn't tell, but Isaac could. He hadn't mentioned it because they'd agreed that their relationship would be friends with benefits. Isaac might want something more serious and committed, but Savannah didn't. In her mind, Mia wasn't a part of the deal. But she was to Isaac.

Even though they had said they weren't going to have a romantic relationship, things had shifted between them. At least, on his part. He was falling in love with Savannah and wanted to build a life with her. She didn't seem any different than before. Well, that wasn't entirely accurate. She had definitely seemed to come out of her shell. She was more fun. More bubbly and definitely less somber.

They hadn't gotten to the benefits part of the relationship, but he didn't know how long he could hold out. His desire was raging out of control, and he was one hot kiss from blowing his plan. Only fear that Savannah would toss him aside after she'd gotten her fill of him kept him from making love to her. He'd worry that he'd been slotted in the friend zone if they hadn't spent numerous evenings making out like teenagers.

But he needed to be honest with Savannah about what he was thinking—hoping—might happen between them. He wanted to take the next steps in their relationship—and he didn't mean friends with benefits. He wanted it all. If Savannah couldn't do that, and that meant including Mia, he was going to end things before they got in too deep. Of course, given how strong his feelings were, it might be too late for him.

Isaac knew he was being unfair—after all, he was changing the terms of the relationship after they'd agreed to them. Perhaps he should have been honest about his feelings in the beginning and let the chips fall where they may—but it was too late to go back and do things differently. And no matter how he'd done things, he would have ended up in the same place.

Wanting a future with Savannah and praying that she felt the same.

Until she'd come into his life, Isaac hadn't imagined settling down. Having a serious relationship had been the furthest thing from his mind. But now he was falling in love with a woman who only wanted to have a good time. She was perfect for the Isaac he used to be. Until he'd fallen for Savannah, he'd never understood why women tried to change a man. Well, it made perfect sense to him now. Love made wise people do foolish things.

And he was about to add one more foolish thing to his tally.

"Since we're not going to eat your friend Nemo, how about we pick up Mia from my parents' and I make something for the three of us? We could even get Scout and let him hang out with us."

Savannah's smile tightened and he knew that she was struggling to keep it in place. "I don't know. Maybe we should just call it a day."

"She's not going anywhere, you know."

Savannah didn't pretend to not know who he was talking about. "I know. But this was never that type of relationship. It's not what we agreed to."

"I understand," he said softly. "But things happen. And in this case, our feelings grew. Changed. I get that is not what you intended, but can you honestly tell me that you don't care for me?"

"Of course I do. We're friends. Good friends.

Just like we said we would be. What we haven't done is indulge in our benefits." She laughed, but it sounded forced.

"You know as well as I do what that term means. Friendship—real friendship—is rarely a part of the deal. It's simply a way to have your physical needs met without making a commitment to the other person. And more often than not, one of the parties ends up feeling hurt and used. Angry."

"I'm definitely starting to feel like you did a little bait-and-switch on me. Be honest. You never intended for this relationship to be casual, Isaac. Did you?" She slammed her hands on her hips.

"What I can honestly say is that as I got to know you, I wanted more from you. At the time, I wasn't sure what that more was."

"And now?" Her voice shook and she stood stock-still, as if preparing herself for a blow.

He looked directly into her eyes. "Now I know I want more than to be your friend."

"Lovers?"

"Yes. But not just that. I want a future with you."

"What if I can't give you that?" she whispered.

"What if you can? I'm the one at risk of being hurt. And I'm willing to take that risk. Are you?"

Was she? Savannah didn't know. Once, the answer would have been a resounding no. A few weeks ago, she wouldn't even be having this debate. But that was before she'd really gotten to know Isaac. Before he'd made her begin to feel again. Before he'd brought her back into the world. Despite her best efforts to protect herself, the wall she'd constructed around her heart had begun to crumble. Before long, it would only be a useless pile of rubble.

She should say no. But somehow, when she hadn't been paying attention, a seed of hope had sprouted inside her. A hope for a future that wasn't solitary. A future that could include love and happiness.

"What are you asking of me?"

"I'm asking for what you can give. Nothing more."

He made it sound so simple when it was anything but.

"And if I can't give it all?"

"What if you can?"

"Don't do that, Isaac. That's not fair. I need to know what you'll do if I can't give you everything that you want. What if I can't be what you want for Mia?"

"Then I'll walk away." His voice was low but firm. "I can't allow her to be hurt."

His words caused a pang in her heart. "I don't like it, but I understand."

"So...what are you saying?"

She took several labored breaths, but couldn't get rid of the tension in her body. Or the dread she couldn't shake that she was making a huge mistake. Was she going to do this? Apparently so. "I guess we should get Mia and Scout and eat some of those steaks."

"It's Betsy."

"What's Betsy."

"Our lunch."

She punched him in the arm. He laughed so hard she was surprised he didn't fall over. "You are not funny at all. Keep it up and we'll have to switch to chicken."

"Not Chester."

They laughed as they went to the house to pick up Mia.

They knocked on the kitchen door and stepped inside. Michelle was sitting on the family room floor and Mia was lying on her back. Michelle was playing "This Little Piggy" with the baby's feet. Mia laughed loudly as her grandmother tugged on her toes.

Michelle smiled at Savannah and Isaac. "I didn't expect you back so soon."

"It turns out that Savannah isn't a fan of fishing."

"It's not for everybody," Michelle said.

"Eeee-eeee," Mia said, demanding her grandmother's attention.

"That's right." She tickled Mia's toes. "'This little piggy went wee, wee, wee, all the way home.'"

"What he means is that I didn't like the idea of eating Nemo," Savannah said, poking fun at herself.

Isaac dropped a hand over her shoulder and gave her an affectionate smile that had her stomach flip-flopping. "She actually named the fish that she caught."

"I see." Michelle smiled as if she saw more than what they were saying.

"So whatever you do, don't let her near any of the cows that we take to market. You know, like the little piggy."

"What?" Savannah asked, looking up at him. "The little piggy was going to market."

"Exactly."

"To shop."

"Not exactly."

"Oh." She thought about it. "*Oh*. Well, thanks for ruining bacon for me, too."

Isaac laughed. "You can continue to think of it your way if that makes you feel better. That little pig is pushing that shopping cart around filling it with cheese and vegetables."

"It's too late to unring that bell."

"Well, don't say I didn't try. Mom, we're going to eat at home, so I came to get Mia."

Michelle picked up the baby and walked over to them. When Mia saw Isaac, she strained against Michelle's hold and held out her arms to him. He took his child and held her in the air for a minute before lowering her and holding her against his chest. Mia rambled a few sentences and then looked at Isaac, as though waiting for his response.

"You don't say," Isaac said.

Mia babbled in reply. Once she'd had the final word, she turned and looked at Savannah. She flashed a dimpled smile and then held out her arms.

Isaac glanced at Savannah.

Despite the feelings churning her insides, she had made a promise to try to open her heart to Mia. And really, that wasn't so hard to do. So she took the baby from Isaac. She closed her eyes at the familiar feel of a child held against her breast. Mia didn't weigh as much as Tony had, but her slightness and her warm body had a massive effect on Savannah. She didn't know how long she would be able to hold back the emotions that began to barrage her. She closed her eyes for a moment in an attempt to still herself. A yank on her ear had her opening them.

"Ow." Mia was tugging on Savannah's earring. How had she forgotten how much babies grabbed anything within their grasp. Savannah reached up to remove the bauble at the same time that Isaac moved to loosen Mia's fingers. There was a brief tussle and Savannah knew exactly how Nemo had felt on the line; once more she was glad that she'd freed him.

After a few painful moments, Savannah managed to unclasp the earring, leaving it clutched in Mia's hand. Naturally, the child brought the earring to her mouth, but Savannah pulled her hand away before she could succeed. Isaac pried the piece of jewelry from his daughter's hand and slid it into his pocket. Mia let out a howl and Michelle popped a pacifier into her mouth. Mia smiled and then lay her head on Savannah's shoulder. Disaster averted, although Savannah's heart was still pounding.

They said goodbye to Michelle and then got into the SUV. Fortunately, the ride to the cabin was short.

"See you in a few," she said as she got out of the SUV. As she stepped inside, she released a breath. As she showered off the grime from their time at the pond, she gave herself a little pep talk. "Don't fret. You'll get wrinkles. And heaven forbid your face freeze like that. It's only for a few hours. Surely you can make it through that."

She gave herself the second verse of the talk while she drove to Isaac's house.

"Come on in," he called when she rang the bell.

Scout heard Isaac's voice and began to pull on the leash. Squaring her shoulders as if readying for battle and inhaling, Savannah opened the door, stepped inside and looked around.

Isaac was walking toward her, wiping his hands on a dish towel. "Perfect timing. I just put the steaks on the grill."

"Where's Mia?" She hadn't meant to ask that, but the words burst right out of her mouth.

"On the deck," Isaac said, leading her through the house. "She's in her playpen, but I don't want to leave her alone for too long."

They stepped outside and Mia dropped the cloth book she was holding, held up her arms and began bouncing on her bottom.

"You don't have to pick her up," Isaac said. "I fed her when we got home, so she hasn't been in there more than five minutes. Not to mention that she was perfectly content in there until she saw you."

Savannah appreciated the out that Isaac was giving her, but she didn't take it. She'd never been a fan of playpens, although she had used one with Tony when she'd had no other option. But more than that, she cared for Isaac—perhaps more than she should—and she wanted to give their relationship a fair chance. That meant opening herself up to Mia.

"I don't mind." Savannah stooped down and held out her arms. "Come on, sweetie."

Mia dropped on all fours and raced over to Savannah. She scooped her up and moved to sit on a chair, Mia on her lap. She'd prepared for the small hands by removing her jewelry and pulling her hair back into a ponytail. Mia was content to play with her toes and say *wee wee*.

"She really likes that nursery rhyme," Savannah said to Isaac.

He turned the two steaks on the grill and then

shut the top. "I know. I read to her every night, but this is the first rhyme that has stuck with her."

"Tony used to love nursery rhymes."

"What was he like?" Isaac sat across from her, looked deep into her eyes and gave her his undivided attention.

"He was a real sweetheart. I think he would have grown up to be a scientist or an engineer. He was so inquisitive. Always wanted to know how things worked. Why did balloons fly away when you let go of the string? Where did they go? Why couldn't they come back down? How did toasters make bread hot? Or what-ifs. What if the wind stopped blowing? What if you could make a house out of cheese?"

Her voice broke on the last word and she took a moment to gather herself. While she did that, Isaac placed the steaks on plates, added potatoes and salad, and then set a plate in front of her. She set Mia in her highchair and then picked up her fork.

She half expected Isaac to change the subject, but once more, he surprised her.

"He sounds like a great kid," he said, sitting across from her.

"The best."

"It's not fair that you lost him so young, but it sounds like he brought you so much joy and love while he was here."

"Yes." There was no love like that of a child. It was so pure. Unconditional. Suddenly, she felt like telling Isaac more about Tony so he would know how special her child was. After a clumsy start, she launched into stories about his firsts. His first word. First step. His first haircut. How he'd tried to put the hair back onto his head. She laughed as she told funny stories as well as touching ones.

Isaac listened attentively, making comments when appropriate. When she was done, she felt wrung out but happy. She'd done what she'd never believed possible. Remembered him with smiles and laughter. Tony had been a great kid—a happy kid— and deserved to be remembered that way.

She looked down and was surprised that she'd cleaned her plate while they'd talked.

She glanced over at Mia. The baby's head bobbed and she closed her eyes. Then she jerked her head up and looked around.

Isaac shook his head. "She's so worried she might miss something."

Savannah laughed. "Let me help you clear the table so you can get that little one to bed for her nap. But not too long, or she won't sleep through the night."

"Trust me, I've learned my lesson."

In under ten minutes, they'd loaded the dishwasher and put away the leftovers. They sat together on the living room couch and Savannah leaned her head against his shoulder. Although it was only midafternoon, she was wiped out. Talking about

Tony had felt good even though it had left her emotionally drained.

"Tired?' Isaac asked.

She nodded. "It's not even four and I'm worn-out."

"You've had an emotional day."

"Thanks for letting me talk about my son."

"Anyone worth loving is worth remembering."

"I know."

"I enjoyed your stories. Feel free to talk about him—or Darren—anytime you want."

"Thank you," she said softly. "And thank you for a wonderful afternoon. I really enjoyed myself."

"Ditto."

She yawned. "I need to get going. I could use a nap myself."

"I know." He cupped her chin, lifting her face to his.

Her breath stalled in her throat as they stared into each other's eyes. Then he caressed her cheek and, ever so slowly, lowered his face to hers. He kissed her softly. Gently. As if he knew that her emotions churned near the surface. After a second, he ended the kiss and leaned his forehead against hers. "Call me when you get home."

"I'm only going next door."

"I know. Call me anyway."

Savannah nodded.

Isaac walked Savannah to the door and stood

on the porch while Savannah let Scout into the car. As she drove away, she knew that something had transpired between them, and she would never be the same.

She just wished she was certain it was a good thing.

Chapter Thirteen

Savannah woke up the following Saturday feeling optimistic. She and Isaac were taking Mia to the park to play and then later to see a puppet show. Miles and Jillian were bringing their children, Benji and Lilliana, so Mia would have other kids to play with.

The past few days had been bumpy, to say the least, but she'd hung in there. She had begun to give her feelings free rein and had been all the happier for it. True, there had been times when she'd panicked about how happy she was and how strong her feelings had become, and had backed away. But she'd always come around.

Allowing herself to become comfortable with Mia had been a bit of a challenge. Mia was vulnerable to so many dangers in the world. So many things could go wrong, and Savannah had to work hard not to obsess over them. But Mia was such a sweetheart that it was impossible to resist her for long.

Just yesterday, Mia had taken a few steps on her own. She'd been using the furniture to cruise around the room for a while, but she'd actually walked from Isaac, who'd been standing at the door, to Savannah, who'd been sitting on the floor near the sofa. Mia had clapped her hands and immediately plopped onto her diapered bottom. Savannah had been filled with immense joy and pride. Instinctively, she'd swept Mia into her arms and hugged her. Isaac had held them both in his arms, and a feeling of rightness had filled her.

Then, afraid of how perfect everything felt, she'd pulled away.

Two steps forward and one step backward.

There was a knock on her front door and then it opened.

"Ready?" Isaac asked, stepping inside. He had Mia in his arms. When Mia spotted Savannah, she immediately held out her arms.

"Absolutely." Savannah took Mia and kissed her chubby cheeks. Savannah loved snuggling Mia close. Mia loved it too, and would stay in Savannah's embrace for several moments before pushing to get down so that she could go in search of adventures. And Scout. "Yes. Would you grab my purse for me?"

Isaac nodded, grabbed the bag, and then the three of them prepared to leave. Scout whined to go.

"Next time, buddy," Isaac said, rubbing the dog.

"He'll be fine. He ran around outside for hours, so he should be ready for a break. Besides, he has his toys if he gets bored."

Scout looked at Isaac. "Sorry. She's the boss." He gave the dog one last rub and then followed Savannah down the front stairs.

Isaac and Savannah talked quietly as they drove to town. The day was perfect, and she was looking forward to spending time in the park. When they arrived, she took Mia from her car seat while Isaac grabbed the diaper bag, blanket and other items they'd need for the day. As they got near the swings, she recalled the night she and Isaac had come here. Dancing together under the moonlit sky. Kissing. It had been heavenly. She'd relived that night many times in her dreams. Now there was a chance it could be repeated in her reality.

Mia clapped her hands when she spotted the baby swing. "Wing?"

"Yes. You're going to swing." Savannah set Mia in the seat and then gave it a little push. Mia gurgled happily and then wiggled her body.

Isaac's phone rang and he answered it. When he ended the call, he looked over at her. "That was

Miles. He and Jillian just got here with Benji and Lilliana. They're on their way over."

"Okay." She'd spent a bit of time with Jillian and Miles over the past weeks and Savannah liked the other couple immensely. Being around Benji was becoming easier. He was a quiet little boy. So different from Tony but sweet in his own way.

A few minutes later, the kids raced over and hopped on the swings. "Push us, Uncle Isaac," Lilliana commanded.

"You got it, boss lady."

Isaac stood between the swings, alternately pushing Lilliana and Benji.

"I see they put you to work," Miles said as he and Jillian approached, holding hands and looking very much in love.

"Easiest job I've had all week."

"I don't doubt it," Miles said. "Something is bothering Nathan, that's for sure."

"I wish he'd work it out before he runs me into the ground." Nathan had begun running the ranch's day-to-day operations with their father.

"No talk about work," Jillian said. "This is family day."

Family day. The words chilled Savannah. Was that what they were? A family? She hadn't signed up for that. Although she and Isaac had grown closer and she loved having him in her life, he and Mia couldn't be her family. Darren and Tony were her family. Their deaths hadn't changed that. As such, that meant Isaac and Mia couldn't be. You couldn't replace family.

"Are you okay?" Isaac asked, stepping up beside her. He had a concerned expression on his face.

"I'm fine," she said, continuing to push Mia's swing. She wasn't fine, but she would keep that information to herself. The last thing she wanted was to ruin this outing for everyone.

The kids swung for twenty minutes before it was time to head over to the stage where the puppet show would take place. Others soon joined them, and the area grew more crowded. The air buzzed with excited chatter. Savannah tried to calm her nerves, but she couldn't rid herself of the sense of dread that threatened to consume her. This was the most people she'd been around since she'd come to Aspen Creek. The most children she'd been around. Despite being outside, she felt boxed in.

They spread their blankets, and Savannah set Mia on her lap. Mia started to squirm, so Savannah set her in front of her. Mia immediately crawled over to the next blanket and sat beside Benji and Lilliana.

Savannah reached for Mia.

"What are you doing?" Isaac asked.

"She's too far away."

"No, she's not. She's only a couple of feet away. She'll be fine."

Savannah knew she was being ridiculous, but she couldn't help it. Although the weather was perfect, she was suddenly cold. She ordered herself to pay attention to the puppets even though she knew she'd never be able to follow the plot. Benji and Lilliana laughed at the antics of the dog puppet, and Mia mimicked them. Jillian and Miles attempted to draw Savannah into conversation, but she was too uneasy to make meaningful contributions.

Finally, the show was over and everyone began to get to their feet. Lilliana and Benji stood and then tried to help Mia stand. Savannah watched, paralyzed, as Mia wobbled. She reached out just as Mia fell on her face. Mia inhaled a long breath and then let out a loud scream.

"No," Savannah cried. She grabbed Mia into her arms, squeezing her tight and kissing her cheek. A knot appeared on the child's forehead. Savannah trembled and her legs shook.

Benji and Lilliana looked on in dismay, clinging to each other's hands. "Sorry, Mia."

Isaac came up behind Savannah and looked over her shoulder at Mia. "She must have landed on a rock."

"She's bleeding." Savannah heard the accusation in her voice. *He* was the one who'd let Mia sit with the other kids. Savannah had wanted to keep Mia on her lap where she would have been safe.

"Just a little. She'll be okay. Let me take her."

Isaac tried to take Mia from Savannah's arms. Mia screeched and clung tighter to Savannah. "Nooo. Mama. Mama. Mama."

Mama. The word tore through Savannah's heart, leaving ripped shreds of flesh in its wake. *Mama.* She was Tony's mama. Not Mia's. And yet her heart was pounding with fear.

She couldn't do this. She couldn't open herself up to this kind of pain again. This was a simple bump on the head, but she knew it could have been worse. And if it had been, she knew that she would never get over it. No matter how much she cared for Isaac and Mia, she couldn't put herself out there again. But she couldn't hand Mia off and run away when the child was in such obvious distress. She rubbed Mia's back, comforting the little girl until her sobs became hiccups. Then Mia put her thumb in her mouth and lay her head against Savannah's shoulder.

Jillian and Miles approached, and Isaac waved them away, so they picked up the blankets and the other scattered belongings. They piled Isaac's things and then took their kids by the hands, leading them off.

Isaac seemed to know that Savannah was overwhelmed and tried once more to take Mia into his arms.

"No," Mia protested, keeping a firm grip on Savannah's top.

"It's okay," Savannah said, although nothing would ever be okay again.

"Let's forget about lunch and head home."

Savannah nodded and let Isaac guide them from the park. Once they were inside the SUV, he drove home. Isaac tried once to make conversation, but Savannah was too overwrought to hold up her end, so they rode to her cabin in uncomfortable silence. After a while, he put in a CD of children's songs that he'd broken down and bought.

When they arrived at the cabin, he parked and started to turn off the engine. Savannah stopped him. "I need some time alone. And I think Mia would feel better at home."

"Mia's fine, as you can see. Besides, you're the one she wants."

And that was the problem. This was exactly the situation she'd been trying to avoid. "Still, I don't think this is a good idea."

"What?" He spun and looked at her. "Coming into your house? Or something else. Because if we're going to have a talk about something serious, a car isn't the place to do it."

He was right. The sooner she ended this…whatever it was they were doing…the sooner she would have her life back. "Fine. Come on in. But don't think you're going to change my mind."

"Since I have no idea what you're talking about,

I don't know whether your mind needs to be changed."

Trust Isaac to be all calm and reasonable. Any other time she would appreciate those attributes. Now she resented him for his easygoing way when she was barely hanging on.

Once they were inside, Isaac set Mia on the floor. She cruised over to Scout. When the dog saw her, he sat up.

"Oh no. There's been enough adventure for one day," Savannah said. She opened the back door and pointed. "Out, Scout."

Scout whined and then slunk out the door and down the stairs.

"Out?" Mia asked as she toddled behind the dog.

"Not you. You're staying inside with us." Isaac scooped her up and then gave her one of the toys he'd left for her to play with when she was visiting. Mia grabbed it enthusiastically and pushed against his chest. He set her down and then looked at Savannah. "I figure we have ten good minutes before she gets bored."

"It won't take me that long to say what I need to say."

"Okay."

"I don't know where to start." Now that she had his attention, she was at a loss for words. She walked to the window and stared outside. Scout had gotten over his disappointment and was chasing a squirrel around the yard.

"I can't do this anymore." She turned from the window and waved her hand between them, including Mia in the mix.

"Can't do what?"

"Be with you. Become a part of your lives. Spending time with you was a mistake. Getting close to Mia. And to you." At the sound of her name, Mia looked up and smiled before turning her attention back to her toy truck. "All of it was wrong. And now it has to stop."

"Why?"

"Because I'm not her mother." And it was wrong to let the little girl believe that she was.

"And she called you mama," he said slowly. Softly.

"Yes."

"Technically, I'm not her father, and she calls me dada."

"That's different. You signed up for that. I didn't."

"I thought you agreed to try."

"Well, it's not working for me, so I want to stop."

"And do what? Go back to your isolated life where you don't let anyone in? What kind of a life is that?"

"It's the life that I choose to live."

"But you're *not* living. You're hiding from life. You're clinging to the past. I know your husband

and son loved you, but they're gone. And they're not coming back."

She turned away from his painful words, and he grasped her shoulders, forcing her to look at him. "Savannah, I told you I'd always be honest with you, so I'm sorry if my words hurt you. I really am." His eyes were intense. Pleading. "But I'm here. Mia's here. We love you and we know that if you open your heart to us, you can love us too. That you can be just as happy as you were before."

The picture he painted sounded good. Too good, so she shoved it away and hardened her heart. "You can't replace them. You can't make me forget them simply because they're gone."

"I know that. And I would never try to. You loved them and they are a part of you. But there is more to you than the past. There's a future waiting to be lived and enjoyed. A present where you are loved. All you have to do is reach out and I'll do the rest."

She folded her arms across her breasts. "I've made my decision. It's over between us. For the present and the future. Now please, take Mia and leave."

"So that's it?" He looked at her and shook his head in disgust. "Fine. We'll leave. And you can keep counting the days you've lived without your family. But from now on, don't think of it as days you've lived without love. Because you *are* loved.

By me. By Mia. You just chose to turn away from that love.

"If it were just me, I would fight to make you see what you're missing out on. Maybe even beg. And I'd make myself happy with whatever crumbs you threw my way. But I can't teach my daughter to beg for love. That's where I draw the line."

Isaac crossed the room and picked up Mia. She grinned at him and patted his cheek. "Dada."

"That's right, baby. I'm your daddy."

Isaac didn't bother to look at Savannah as he left. Mia reached for her, but Isaac turned his body away so they couldn't touch. Apparently, he wasn't going to give her a chance to say goodbye to his daughter. He slammed the door behind him as he left and then jogged down the stairs.

Savannah watched from the corner of her window while Isaac settled Mia into her car seat and then got behind the wheel of the SUV. She didn't look away until the vehicle was no longer visible.

As the tears streamed down her face, she reminded herself that this was what she wanted. It was for the best.

So why was she suddenly so miserable?

That feeling greeted Savannah every day for the next week. As if in sync with her mood, the weather had taken a turn for the gloomy and rained consistently. Scout hadn't picked up on her feelings and wanted to play as much as ever. In between downpours, Savannah put on her boots and dutifully went out into the yard with him.

They stepped outside and, predictably, he picked up his ball and brought it over to her.

She took it from him and threw it unenthusiastically. It wasn't as if she had anything else to do. He scampered away happily, splashing mud all over himself. She stepped back, but it was too late. He'd gotten her all muddy too. It looked like both of them were going to need baths.

Savannah tried to focus on Scout and his happiness, but she couldn't shake the cloud of misery following her around. She made herself face the truth. She missed Isaac and Mia, and had from the moment they'd driven out of sight. She told herself that she'd simply gotten used to having them around, that it wouldn't be hard to get used to them not being there. Then she would be fine. Now she admitted that she'd lied.

It started to rain again and she hustled Scout into the house. She gave him a bath and then took a shower of her own. With nothing else to do, she grabbed the TV remote and sat on the sofa. She'd been avoiding this room since the breakup. It was the last place she'd seen Isaac and sitting there made his absence more real. Something poked her back and she moved the throw pillow. One of Mia's toys. Savannah had packed up Mia's belongings and set them on the porch the day after she'd told Isaac to get lost. She'd texted him to come get them and he had grabbed the box at some time, not bothering to ring the doorbell to let her know he'd come by.

She held the stuffed toy for a moment before setting it on the coffee table, no longer interested in watching TV. Perhaps baking cookies would cheer her up. But she remained seated.

It had been nine days since Isaac had walked out on her. Nine long days filled with nothing but sorrow and loneliness. The thought brought her up short. *Why was she counting the days since she and Isaac had ended things between them? Why was she keeping track that way?* Their relationship hadn't been that serious. She'd ended it on her terms. Hadn't she? Surely she wasn't equating his absence with Darren and Tony's.

Slightly panicked, she raced to her bedroom and pulled out a small chest where she'd put all of the cards and letters Darren had given her over the years. She hadn't been able to read them since he'd died. Hadn't even touched them. The pain had been too great. But now she needed to see the words that he'd written so she could regain the closeness they'd once shared.

Darren had loved writing letters and a good deal of their courtship had occurred when he'd put pen to paper. She set aside the cards and immediately went to the letters. They were in chronological order, and she started with the oldest first. She opened the envelope, unfolded the paper and caressed Darren's bold penmanship. As she read his letter—the first he'd ever written to her—tears filled her eyes.

The letter was filled with his hopes and dreams. For himself. For her. For them. As she read, her heart overflowed. He'd loved her so much even then. Then she read his final words.

> *What I want most for you is happiness. Even if I am not a part of it. I wish you a long life filled with joy. If you have that, I'll have everything that I need.*

She cried as she folded the paper. He had wanted her to be happy. She'd known that. Even if he wasn't there to share her happiness. True, when he'd written the letter, he'd been talking about if things hadn't worked out between them as a couple. And things hadn't worked out for them. He'd died. But after reading his words, she knew that he wouldn't want her to mourn him forever. He'd always tried to make her happy. He would want her to be happy now.

He'd be so disappointed that she had stopped living when he and Tony died. If he were here, he'd tell her to let Isaac and Mia into her life. To love them and let them love her. Isaac wasn't trying to replace them. She knew that. Isaac knew she would always love Darren and Tony. But now she knew she could love Isaac and Mia too.

She just hoped she wasn't too late.

* * *

It had finally stopped raining. Thank goodness. Isaac wasn't sure he would be able to stand another gray day. It was as if nature had known he was crying and empathized with him. Today the sun was shining, and he and Mia were enjoying time outside. She had mastered walking and he was able to watch her toddle across the floor without his heart being firmly lodged in his throat.

Now they held hands as they walked across the patio. She stooped down to look at a worm slithering across the ground. When she reached for it, Isaac grabbed her hand. He didn't want her to become squeamish about bugs, but he didn't want this poor creature to be squished to death either. And he certainly didn't want Mia to try to eat it. Mia rose and continued to wander across the path, looking for the next interesting thing.

He heard a throat being cleared and turned around. *Savannah.* His heart jumped and started to race. It had been ten long days since he'd seen her. Ten long days since he'd held her in his arms. It seemed like years. Now she was standing in front of him, looking as beautiful as ever. Many questions raced through his mind, but he couldn't find the voice to ask even one of them.

Mia saw Savannah, dropped Isaac's hand and then began to waddle as fast as her little legs could go. "Mama."

"No," he said, stirring himself. He took two steps and then scooped Mia into his arms. Mia struggled, but he didn't put her down.

Isaac looked at Savannah, forcing a hard edge into his voice so it wouldn't betray his feelings. "Why are you here?"

"I wanted to talk."

"You made yourself perfectly clear. I can't imagine that there is anything left to say."

She looked at Mia, who had stopped struggling and was now tugging on Isaac's locks. He would rather endure the discomfort of having his hair yanked out at the roots than rehash the past with Savannah. Apparently, both things were going to happen at once.

"There is one thing."

"What?" He managed to free his hair from Mia's grasp and set her on her feet.

Savannah looked uneasy and, for the briefest moment, his heart ached for her. He wanted to comfort her, tell her everything would be okay, but he had Mia to think of. Her well-being was more important than his broken heart. And Savannah had never wanted a relationship, so she was getting what she needed. Who was he to say how she should live her life? If she was happy, he was happy for her. But she didn't look happy. And why was she here if she wanted them out of her life?

"I read some letters that Darren wrote to me long ago. Reading them felt like he was talking to me."

"I'm happy for you. This means you don't actually have to let him go."

She hesitated. "His letter made clear that he wanted me to be happy even if it wasn't with him. That, no matter what, he would want me to live. To love. The same way that you do."

He wanted to take her in his arms, but he held back. He needed to be certain that she was sure of her feelings. He couldn't have her backing away if things got too real for her. Not for his daughter's sake. Not for his own. "What are you saying?"

"I'm saying that I love you. That I love Mia. That I want us to be together. It took me a while to figure it out, but living with fear is no way to live. I don't want that life anymore. I don't want to live without love. I don't want to live without you and Mia."

Isaac felt a rush of emotion in his chest. "You don't have to. I can't promise that nothing bad will happen to any of us, but I promise to love you with my entire heart."

"I promise you the same."

They raced to each other, clinging tight for several minutes.

"One more thing," Savannah said, easing out of his arms. "I have a gift for you."

Her love was the only gift he needed. "Really? What is it?"

She crossed over to the table and picked up a bag she'd set there then walked back over to him. She reached into the bag, pulled out a calendar and opened it to this month. A big one was written on today's date.

He looked at her. "What does this mean?"

"It marks the first day of the rest of our lives. The first of many we'll have to love each other. From now on, this is how I intend to mark my days. By how many days we spend loving each other."

He pulled her close and kissed her. "That sounds like a plan I can get behind."

Mia toddled over and grabbed their knees. Savannah picked her up, hugged her close. Isaac wrapped the two of them in his arms. His family.

Savannah and Isaac knew that life could hold tragedies, but it also held joy. And, most importantly, it held love.

* * * * *

Don't miss Nathan's story,
The next installment of Kathy Douglass's new
miniseries
Aspen Creek Bachelors
coming soon to Harlequin Special Edition!
And look for Miles and Jillian's story,
Valentines for the Rancher,
Available now!

#2977 SELF-MADE FORTUNE
The Fortunes of Texas: Hitting the Jackpot • by Judy Duarte
Heiress Gigi Fortune has the hots for her handsome new lawyer! Harrison Vasquez may come from humble beginnings, but they have so much fun—in and out of bed! If only she can convince him their opposite backgrounds are the perfect ingredients for a shared future...

#2978 THE MARINE'S SECOND CHANCE
The Camdens of Montana • by Victoria Pade
The worst wound Major Dalton Camden ever received was the day Marli Abbott broke his heart. Now the fate of Marli's brother is in his hands...and Marli's back in town, stirring up all their old emotions. This time, they'll have to revisit the good *and* the bad to make their second-chance reunion permanent.

#2979 LIGHTNING STRIKES TWICE
Hatchet Lake • by Elizabeth Hrib
Newly single Kate Cardiff is in town to care for her sick father and his ailing ranch. The only problem? Annoying—and annoyingly sexy—ranch hand Nathan Prescott. Nathan will use every tool at his disposal to win over love-shy Kate. Starting with his knee-weakening kisses...

#2980 THE TROUBLE WITH EXES
The Navarros • by Sera Taíno
Dr. Nati Navarro's lucrative grant request is under review—by none other than her ex Leo Espinoza. But Leo is less interested in holding a grudge and much more interested in exploring their still-sizzling connection. Can Nati's lifelong dream include a career *and* romance this time around?

#2981 A CHARMING SINGLE DAD
Charming, Texas • by Heatherly Bell
How dare Rafe Reyes marry someone else! Jordan Del Toro knows she should let bygones be bygones. But when a wedding brings her face-to-face with her now-divorced ex—and his precious little girl—Jordan must decide if she wants revenge... or a new beginning with her old flame.

#2982 STARTING OVER AT TREVINO RANCH
Peach Leaf, Texas • by Amy Woods
Gina Heron wants to find a safe refuge in her small Texas hometown—*not* in Alex Trevino's strong arms. But reuniting with the boy she left behind is more powerful and exhilarating than a mustang stampede. The fiery-hot chemistry is still there. But can she prove she's no longer the cut-and-run type?

Get 4 FREE REWARDS!

We'll send you 2 FREE Books plus 2 FREE Mystery Gifts.

FREE
Value Over
$20

Both the **Harlequin® Special Edition** and **Harlequin® Heartwarming™** series feature compelling novels filled with stories of love and strength where the bonds of friendship, family and community unite.

YES! Please send me 2 FREE novels from the Harlequin Special Edition or Harlequin Heartwarming series and my 2 FREE gifts (gifts are worth about $10 retail). After receiving them, if I don't wish to receive any more books, I can return the shipping statement marked "cancel." If I don't cancel, I will receive 6 brand-new Harlequin Special Edition books every month and be billed just $5.49 each in the U.S. or $6.24 each in Canada, a savings of at least 12% off the cover price, or 4 brand-new Harlequin Heartwarming Larger-Print books every month and be billed just $6.24 each in the U.S. or $6.74 each in Canada, a savings of at least 19% off the cover price. It's quite a bargain! Shipping and handling is just 50¢ per book in the U.S. and $1.25 per book in Canada.* I understand that accepting the 2 free books and gifts places me under no obligation to buy anything. I can always return a shipment and cancel at any time by calling the number below. The free books and gifts are mine to keep no matter what I decide.

Choose one: ☐ **Harlequin Special Edition**
(235/335 HDN GRJV)
☐ **Harlequin Heartwarming**
Larger-Print
(161/361 HDN GRJV)

Name (please print)

Address   Apt. #

City   State/Province   Zip/Postal Code

Email: Please check this box ☐ if you would like to receive newsletters and promotional emails from Harlequin Enterprises ULC and its affiliates. You can unsubscribe anytime.

Mail to the **Harlequin Reader Service:**
IN U.S.A.: P.O. Box 1341, Buffalo, NY 14240-8531
IN CANADA: P.O. Box 603, Fort Erie, Ontario L2A 5X3

Want to try 2 free books from another series! Call 1-800-873-8635 or visit www.ReaderService.com.

*Terms and prices subject to change without notice. Prices do not include sales taxes, which will be charged (if applicable) based on your state or country of residence. Canadian residents will be charged applicable taxes. Offer not valid in Quebec. This offer is limited to one order per household. Books received may not be as shown. Not valid for current subscribers to the Harlequin Special Edition or Harlequin Heartwarming series. All orders subject to approval. Credit or debit balances in a customer's account(s) may be offset by any other outstanding balance owed by or to the customer. Please allow 4 to 6 weeks for delivery. Offer available while quantities last.

Your Privacy—Your information is being collected by Harlequin Enterprises ULC, operating as Harlequin Reader Service. For a complete summary of the information we collect, how we use this information and to whom it is disclosed, please visit our privacy notice located at corporate.harlequin.com/privacy-notice. From time to time we may also exchange your personal information with reputable third parties. If you wish to opt out of this sharing of your personal information, please visit readerservice.com/consumerchoice or call 1-800-873-8635. **Notice to California Residents**—Under California law, you have specific rights to control and access your data. For more information on these rights and how to exercise them, visit corporate.harlequin.com/california-privacy.

HSEHW22R3

HARLEQUIN
PLUS

Try the best multimedia
subscription service for romance
readers like you!

Read, Watch and Play.

Experience the easiest way to get
the romance content you crave.

Start your **FREE TRIAL** at
<u>www.harlequinplus.com/freetrial</u>.